MIDNIGHT RAIN

In the dark days of the Great Depression, Detective Jack Dunning and his partner Jim Tunney are investigating the deaths of two young boys found on the same stretch of highway in recent weeks. Could their deaths be connected to the disappearance of three girls from the Saguaro Correctional Institution in the isolated Mojave Desert? How does the mysterious Deutschlander Social Club fit into the picture? And Jack's beautiful live-in girlfriend, Angel Doll, has problems of her own when a threatening figure emerges from her troubled past . . .

Books by Arlette Lees
in the Linford Mystery Library:

ANGEL DOLL
CODE OF SILENCE

ARLETTE LEES

MIDNIGHT RAIN

Complete and Unabridged

LINFORD
Leicester

First published in Great Britain in 2014

First Linford Edition
published 2015

A catalogue record for this book is available
from the British Library.

ISBN 978–1–4448–2376–9

Published by
F. A. Thorpe (Publishing)
Anstey, Leicestershire

Set by Words & Graphics Ltd.
Anstey, Leicestershire
Printed and bound in Great Britain by
T. J. International Ltd., Padstow, Cornwall

This book is printed on acid-free paper

Prologue

Penelope Hanover steps from her bungalow beyond the main complex and breathes
in the chilly April air. Three miles distant,
backlit by an overblown moon, the boulder-
strewn Alamillo Escarpment, with its volcanic
chimneys and sharp pinnacles, rolls for
twenty miles toward the Nevada border.

Once used as a hideout by outlaws, more
people have ventured into the Escarpment
than have returned. An old wagon trail
accommodates a car for a short distance,
but it's not recorded on any map. Treasure
hunters unearth Spanish coins, arrowheads,
pottery and broken wagon wheels . . . even
the occasional human bone. For Penny,
who's always lived in the city, Saguaro is a
great adventure.

Ignoring warnings about tarantulas and

scorpions, Penny walks down the moon-silvered path beneath a sky of cartwheeling constellations. It's a lovely night to spread her wings and enjoy her newfound freedom.

Penelope's mother didn't want her working with delinquents, especially since she'd been offered a respectable teaching position close to home. 'Why bother with bad girls who will only end up in Tehachapi in a year or two?' she'd said, Tehachapi being the correctional institution for women. But getting out from beneath her mother's oppressive thumb was the whole point of moving this far from home.

Last year she'd moved from the family home into her first apartment, but when she caught Mom inspecting her sheets for evidence of male guests, it was the last straw. She had nothing to hide, but she was tired of being scrutinized like a bug under glass.

Penny hears conversation coming from the bungalow of the girl from payables/receivables and wonders who she's talking with at this hour. Her name is Hedy and although she's brilliant with numbers, she's cool and aloof, like she thinks she's better than everyone else. Penny and the other teachers on the staff, who were once welcoming to the outsider, have given up trying to befriend her.

Curious as a cat, she creeps to the open window. She stands on tiptoe and sees Hedy sitting at what appears to be a shortwave radio, something Penny has only seen in news reels from the Great War. A man's voice breaks through the incessant static: 'Lebens-born . . . Bundesrepublik Deuchland . . . Geheimer Staatspolizei . . . Blut . . . Reinheit . . . Mangel,' each word as hard and heavy as a wooden shoe. Hedy replies in the same guttural tongue.

When Hedy shifts in her chair, Penny drops to a crouch below the windowsill. She hears the names of three young inmates who'd gone missing from Saguaro: Patty Gregson, Velma Becker, Sarah Levin. The man on the shortwave says: 'Gut, gut, gut!'

Penny's back cramps. She adjusts her position and a rock crunches beneath her heel. The conversation inside the room terminates abruptly. A chair scrapes across the floor and Penny's heart jolts in her chest. She jumps to her feet and makes a reckless dash for her bungalow . . . crunch . . . crunch . . . crunch. She locks herself inside and leans breathlessly against the closed door, her knees trembling so bad they barely support her weight. She listens until she's certain she hasn't been followed, then giggles nervously like a pickpocket who's made a clean getaway.

She can't believe she's done such a stupid, childish thing. Her mother always said that eavesdroppers deserve what they hear, but Penny isn't sure what she's heard or what it means. Late into the night she lays awake wondering why the man on the other end of the short wave thinks there's something gut . . . gut . . . gut about three missing girls. Although they were different ages and attended different classes, it was assumed the girls ran off together. Sarah, a quiet studious girl, had been a student in Penny's English class, but she didn't know the other two; had never heard their names until they'd vanished.

4

Saguaro Correctional lies in the Mojave Desert in southeastern California and takes its name from the giant candelabra cacti that abound in the area. No high walls or barbed wire surround the premises because the desert itself is more effective than steel bars. Its daytime temperatures often exceed 120 degrees and drop to near-freezing at night. Even if an inmate escaped, where would they go? There's no town for fifty miles in any direction . . . no food . . . no water . . . no gas . . . only rattlesnakes, coyotes and black, ragged-winged vultures.

A car would be the likely means of escape, but none had gone missing the night the girls vanished. There's a lightly traveled highway on the far horizon that flies straight as an arrow across the state line, but even if they reached it, who'd pick up three girls in institutional uniforms, unless of course they were up to no good?

The following morning Penny pins her lacy cameo brooch to the collar of her white blouse and slips her garnet class ring on what will one day be her wedding ring finger. She goes straight to the library and pulls out the German/English dictionary, not ready to dismiss the events of the previous night without further investigation. The Great War is behind them, but in its wake is a xenophobic uneasiness that's hard to shake.

Sleep has washed away the long, complicated words she's tried so hard to remember. As she runs a finger down a list of foreign words, a shadow falls over her shoulder. Wouldn't you know? It's Hedy, the number-cruncher. She tries to appear composed, but there's nothing she can do about the flush that colors her cheeks.

'So, you will be teaching German?' says Hedy. 'Better you should stick with English, no?' Hedy has worked hard to lose her accent, to keep from pronouncing Ws like Vs, but her syntax gives her away.

Hedy smiles and walks away, but it's not a friendly smile. Despite her embarrassment at being found out, Penny stubbornly flips through the pages of the book, recalling a few of the shorter words she'd heard.

Blut. Reinheit. Mangel.
Blood. Purity. Defect.
Taken out of context, the words are meaningless. Disappointed, she slaps the book shut, returns it to the shelf and goes upstairs to teach her English class.

1

Santa Paulina, California
November 1936

I slip from beneath the covers and put a pot of coffee on the hotplate, leaving Angel asleep with her hair wisping over her eyes. We live in 210, a corner room with a bath that overlooks Cork Street in the Little Ireland section of Santa Paulina, California. The street is named after a county in Ireland, not the bottle stopper, but in this neighborhood it goes both ways. My name is Jack Dunning. I've been two years with the S.P.P.D as well as working security here at the Rexford Hotel for my old war buddy, Hank Featherstone.

Wind rattles the window and the furnace clanks from the bowels of the building. The marquee on the movie theater across the street is dark, and black clouds gather along the northern horizon. I watch Angel sleep, her hair still honey-dipped from the summer sun. She's pretty — I mean glow-in-the-dark pretty, like a candle flame in a gold glass bottle. She's also young, young enough to get me busted in jurisdictions where law enforcement has nothing better to do than count on their fingers.

Me? I'm not young — well, not *that* young. I guess you could say I'm in my late prime, reasonably fit, with a steady gun hand. I'm not as fast on my feet as I used to be, but I still have a fist that can crack a cinderblock. I have an even temperament both at home and on the job and although I don't look for trouble, it sometimes tracks me down. I was fifteen years with the Boston P.D. but I couldn't keep the cork in the bottle back then. They allowed me to resign just short of being canned. My family wrote me off as a lost cause, so I hopped a Greyhound and came west. I still drink, but I keep it down to a mild roar and I'm never drunk on the job.

Angel stirs and opens her eyes — long-lashed eyes, blue as rain. She's my reason for getting up in the morning and staying out of the bars at night. As a cop I can be a tough son-of-a-gun, trained in the school of hard knocks on the broken streets of Southie, but when I'm with Angel, I go soft in the knees and hard below the belt. She muffles a yawn and looks toward the window.

'It's awfully dark out there. You think the storm will hit today?' she says.

'The weatherman says today, maybe tomorrow. I'm going to jump in the shower while the coffee's perking.'

'First come here,' she says, moving the covers aside with a sleepy smile, a lock of hair tumbling over one eye. She's all peaches and cream, her thighs silky and smooth. 'I'm perking too,' she says in a whisper.

When I'm committed to a woman I'm in all the way — no games, no playing hard to get. I light two Luckys and carry them to the bed. The sheets carry Angel's warmth and the scent of her dime-store perfume. She takes a cigarette from my fingers, but sets it smoking in the ashtray on the bed stand. There's something she

10

wants more than a cigarette.

I take a long drag, blow the smoke to the side and set my cigarette next to hers. She reaches out and I lower myself on my elbows. I kiss her and bury my face in her hair. It tickles and she laughs. Angel is beautiful inside and out. She's also a girl with a past. Yes, *that* kind of past. You'd never know it. She's sweet and fresh as the day she was born. You'll get the whole story sooner or later . . . or not. I may not have the whole story myself.

I've been hooked on Angel since I got off the Greyhound in the midnight rain with one suitcase, a gun and a few bucks in my pocket. I ducked out of the wind into the Blue Rose Dance Hall, a fancy euphemism for dime-a-dance joint. The room was so full of cigarette smoke you'd swear the building was on fire. Just my kind of place. A mirrorball on the ceiling threw silver darts of light around the room and men wearing everything from zoot suits, to sailor suits, to patched overalls drank bootleg booze from flasks in the dark corners of the room.

I handed all my dance tickets to the girl

11

in the blue silk dress, the only one in the room who'd forgotten the heavy make-up and penciled beauty marks; the one who looked frightened and too young to be out after dark. She said her name was Angel Dahl, but I took it for Doll, and that's the way I still think of her. My Angel Doll. Her hair smelled like roses that night, her mouth like the pink lipstick kiss on a love letter. I folded her in my arms with her head beneath my chin and we danced long and slow to 'Stormy Weather' and a jazz rendition of 'The Shadow Waltz'.

The lights flickered on and off at the end of the last dance. Angel had a little-girl-lost look that got to me, so I walked her through the rain to the Rexford. She had a rented room at the end of the hall, but she spent the night in mine. Later, when we lay smoking in bed, she asked me if I was married. Most men my age are unless they're total screw-ups.

'She's divorcing me,' I said. 'She's back on the east coast where my replacement sleeps on my side of the bed.'

'Did you cheat on her?' she asks. She

says it casually, without judgment.

'Only with Jack Daniels.'

She touched my cheek with her fingertips, a sad smile on her face. 'I've never been with anyone like this before,' she said

I didn't know what to say. I took a drag on my Lucky and watched the purple smoke rise from the tip of my cigarette. The colored lights from the movie marquee cast pink and purple reflections on the ceiling of the room. I wasn't sure what she wanted from me.

'I don't know what that means,' I said.

'Giving myself because I want to.' She said it matter-of-factly, but there was an infinite sadness in her eyes. 'Everything's been taken from me, ever since I was thirteen, ever since my parents died. Axel Teague runs the vice in this town and he runs me too.' A tear balanced on her eyelid and she tried to brush it away before I noticed. 'I'm not asking you to feel sorry for me. I'm just letting you know how it is.'

I whispered in her hair, 'No one's going to run you after tonight. How about we make this the first time for both of us, the only time that counts.' I pulled her close and felt her fear melt away in my arms. We've been together ever since.

A flicker of dry lightning plays on the far horizon and brings me back to the moment. I hear the coffee perking, the early traffic on the street. Angel looks up at me, her face softly feline . . . a little more than kitten . . . a little less than cat. I feel her warm breath on my neck.

I know how to make her purr.

★   ★   ★

I ride to the lobby in the elevator with a few rental aps. Out of six, I've rejected one, the guy who was kicked out of the flophouse by the railroad tracks for rolling derelicts who were more blitzed than he was.

The Rexford, which consists of three floors above the lobby, twenty rooms per floor, isn't the Ritz, but it's clean and well-run and keeps Hank in gambling chips and Cuban cigars. With a few exceptions we cater to single blue-collar men, boxers from the gym, pensioners who fought in the Great War, a few elderly couples and a handful of Mexicans and Dust Bowl refugees who work at the cannery and packing house.

Some of the tenants have misdemeanor warrants in other jurisdictions, or a skeleton or two they'd like to keep from leaping out of the closet, but as long as they pay their rent and don't cause a ruckus they're welcome. For the most part they're a decent bunch, everyone struggling through the Depression, looking for the light at the end of the tunnel.

The lobby looks like a million lobbies in a million towns: reception desk . . . oak woodwork . . . polished hardwood floors. There's a cigarette machine inside the front door, a magazine stand out front, and Kelly Green Cabs at the curb.

The lounge by the front window has comfortable leather couches and chairs on a carpet with the requisite number of cigarette burns. Potted palms fan out at the foot of support pillars and sand buckets bristle with cigarette butts and dead matches. Men are waking up over coffee, cigarettes and newspapers, the radio tuned low to the weather report.

Hank looks up from behind the desk, his bifocals low on his nose, pink scalp showing through his thinning hair. Hank was born in Little Ireland and lived most of his life out of Duffy's Gym, first as welterweight, then as trainer and some-time manager. When the hotel went into foreclosure five years back, he picked it up for back taxes and quit the fight game for good.

'Morning, Hank.'

'Morning, Jack. The weatherman says this could be the big one.'

'Could be.'

'Volunteers are out patching the levy.'

'It's a little late for that.'

Hank holds up a whiskey bottle. 'Eye-opener?'

'Better not.' I put the aps on the desk in front of him. 'This one's a rotten apple. The rest look okay.' He's about to say something when the desk phone rings and he picks it up. He listens, then covers the mouthpiece.

'It's Jim Tunney,' he says. 'That rookie

16

just got hired on is sprawled on the highway with his patrol car off to the side. Jim says if you want to ride shotgun, you've got five minutes to get to the station.'

'Thanks, Hank. Tell him I'm on my way.'

*   *   *

After Jack leaves, Angel sits contentedly in the easy chair, sipping a second cup of coffee with her feet tucked beneath her. On the street below the window a derelict hunches into the collar of his coat and a newspaper flies apart in the wind. Angel leans back and closes her eyes. She can still taste Jack's nicotine kisses and feel where his rough cheek rubbed the sensitive skin of her throat.

Before her parents died in a typhoid epidemic, she'd lived in a modest house in Banning, where her father worked as a mining engineer for a drilling company. She got good grades and took ballet lessons in a little white tutu. The day after her parents' funeral, a man posing as a distant relative showed up at her door. His name was Axel Teague. Angel was thirteen, just a kid. It never occurred to her to ask for credentials or question his veracity.

By the time she was missed, she was hundreds of miles away in Santa Paulina. By then, she knew Teague's plan for her future, which differed greatly from the one she and her parents had aspired to. An escape attempt ended in a concussion and broken arm. Teague said he'd kill her if she tried to escape again.

Angel is happy at the Rexford with Jack. They belong together, two complex people with complicated histories. She can't imagine being with anyone else . . . ever.

The last cigarette in the pack is broken. As she tries piecing it together, there's a knock at the door and she crumbles the tobacco into the ashtray. 'Come on in, Albie,' she says, tightening the sash of her robe and setting her coffee cup on the table next to the chair.

'Mornin', Miss Angel.'

'Morning, Albie.'

Albie delivers the *Santa Paulina Morning Sun*, three cents a copy, a nickel on

18

Sunday. He's an enterprising little squirt with an engaging personality and ready smile. He's smaller than most ten-year-olds; wears saggy overalls and a red cap with the bill turned sideways. He gives Angel the paper. She hands him an extra dime to bring her cigarettes from the machine.

Albie is the closest thing the hotel has to room service. He can hustle up almost anything you need: a magazine . . . cigarettes . . . complimentary coffee from the lobby or take-out from the Memory Lights Café. He can steam a suit, press a shirt, shine shoes . . . anything except run numbers for Toots McGee out of the back room of the Tammany Hall Bar, although the offer is still on the table.

Albie's father, Jake Sherman, is head of the hotel janitorial and housekeeping staff. On Saturday nights he blows a mean sax at Smokey's Barbecue Pit by the river. There was once a Mrs. Sherman, but she left town with a fancy-man in a shark-skin suit and an ace of diamonds in his hatband.

Jake and Albie live in the furnace room, which isn't as bad as it sounds. They have cots in an alcove beneath the ductwork, a bathroom and shower at one end of the basement and a communal laundry with clotheslines stretched across the ceiling. It's warm in winter, cool in summer, and it's free. Those poor folks in the Hooverville on River Road would give anything to have it so good.

Albie returns with cigarettes and Angel gives him a nickel tip to jingle in his pocket with the rest of his morning take.

'Thank you, Miss Angel.'

'You must be rich as Rockefeller,' she says, leaning down to straighten the collar of his shirt.

'I got fifteen dollars in my coffee can.'

'That's a lot of money, Albie. Be sure you keep it in a safe place.'

'Mr. Reese in 320 says if I loan him ten dollars, he'll give me twelve when his ship comes in.'

'Don't you listen to that man, Albie. Mr. Reese's ship went to the bottom in '29. He gets any wise ideas about your money, he'll have Jack to deal with.'

'Yes, ma'am. Jake wants me to bring all them flashlights up from the basement in

case we lose power. You think it's really
going to get that bad?'

'Better to be safe than sorry. Run along
now so I can get dressed.'

⋆   ⋆   ⋆

Around noon Angel goes downstairs wearing a beige raincoat and carrying her blue
umbrella. In the lounge, men sit around
the radio drinking their morning coffee,
ashes growing long on their cigarettes as
they lean close to the speaker.

Cantor Nemschoff, with his long white
beard, is looking more solemn than usual.
'Shhh! Just listen,' he says when Angel
approaches. She takes a seat beside him.
The voice on the radio belongs to Nathaniel
Forsythe, the anchor of the daily news
editorial, 'Up To Date':

'*In July, construction commenced on
the Sachsenhousen Concentration Camp
at Oranienburg, near Berlin. By September 23rd, it housed 1000 inmates labeled
enemies of the state, ordinary citizens
incarcerated without due process: gypsies,
Jews, 7th Day Adventists, Catholics,*

21

intellectuals, the mentally and physically defective, and anyone who questions Nazi authority. Pogroms and mass exterminations are reported in outlying Polish and Russian communities.

'On October 1st, criminal court judges in Berlin took mandatory oaths of allegiance to Hitler. Nazi Minister of Propaganda Joseph Goebbels has banned film criticism, allowing the Nazi-controlled German film industry to pursue its blatantly anti-Semitic rants.

'We're out of time for today, but tune in tomorrow for continuing coverage of The Growing Nazi Threat To The Civilized World. Until then, I am Nathaniel Forsythe reporting.'

The room is suddenly a-murmur with voices, some listeners buying into every word, other thinking something so outlandish couldn't possibly be true.

'Don't you have a brother in Berlin?' says Angel, turning to the cantor.

'Years ago I begged him to bring his family to America, but he didn't vant to valk avay from his successful gallery. He had a Van Gogh, a Kandinsky and a von

Werefkin among other fine paintings. Now, da SS is quartered in his home and da gallery seized.'

'Have you heard from them since this happened?'

'No von knows vat's become of dem. My cousin Moisha, a vell-respected urologist, has lost hospital privileges. My nephew, Schmueli, ousted from university. All Jewish students gone, gone, gone and Schmueli has fled to Paris.'

'I'm so sorry. Isn't a pogrom some kind of riot?'

'It's da organized massacre of an ethnic group. It's vat da Turks did to da Armenians and vat da Germans do to us. It's dere method of confiscating property vithout compensation and viping us from da face of da earth so ve can't tell.'

Angel sits quietly for a moment, trying to take it all in. 'Come up to my room, Cantor. Let me make you a cup of tea.'

He smooths his long white beard and rises shakily onto his cane. 'No tank you, dear. I tink I'll lie down avile. Dese old knees predict rain better den da veaderman.'

Angel rides with him up the elevator and sees him safely to his room. When she returns to the lobby, Hank is behind the desk sorting mail. 'You heard what Forsythe said. Is there going to be another war?' she asks.

'There's *always* going to be another war, but this time Jack and I won't be in it. We beat them s.o.b.s once already. If they're smart, they won't make us do it again.'

2

Officer Jim Tunney is my partner. He was my first friend when I hit town. He's red-Irish with a touch of the old Viking blood. His blue eyes are as pale as drinking water and he has the kind of fair freckled skin you don't parade in the noonday sun.

Soon after we met, he said the S.P.P.D. had never had a bona fide, big-city detective on the force, and after checking me out, Chief Garvey was all for it. I considered telling a whopper about my inglorious departure from the B.P.D. but decided to play it on the square.

'They forced me out in Boston,' I said. 'I couldn't crawl out of the bottle back then. I'm doing better now.' The chief joked that as long as I don't fall off the floor, I haven't reached my limit. I was in like Flynn.

Jim and I streak to the site, where Ted 'Curley' McDaniel is sprawled on the highway near Sparkey's Roadhouse. Only one road can be considered a highway in these parts. Everything else is a street, a dirt road or a cow path. The highway runs from the Tehachapi Mountains in southern California, through the Central Valley and on to points north. When we arrive on the accident scene, the ambulance attendants are splinting Curley's leg for transport to Santa Paulina General, a spacious three-story house that was turned into a rehab center for wounded soldiers of the Great War.

'The s.o.b. plowed right into me,' moans Curley. 'Busted me up pretty bad.'

'I can see that,' says Jim.

The road rash on Curley's face looks like he tried to shave with a road grader. Serpentine tire tracks zigzag across the center line. There's a tread mark on Curley's pants leg and one cowboy boot is missing. It's evident no brakes were applied either before or after the accident. Then again, maybe it wasn't an accident. Maybe someone has it in for him. Who knows, maybe someone is out to get any cop who makes himself an easy target.

'What were you doing outside of your car?' I ask.

'Waving my arms to get the attention of that crazy driver.' — 'crazy' being the operative word here. 'A truck from Cooley's was almost forced into the ditch.'

'Get a description of the vehicle?'

'Green sedan, driver so short only tufts of orangey hair were visible through the steering wheel. Could have been an adult or minor, male or female, a clown or an Irish setter for that matter.'

'After he hit you, which way did he go?'

'Don't know. I was busy spitting gravel out of my teeth.'

'You think you can finish this conversation at the hospital?' says the attendant, strapping Curley onto the stretcher.

Jim turns to me. 'How about I follow them in and get a formal statement?' he says.

'Good idea. I'll bring Curley's car in.'

I climb behind the wheel of McDaniel's black and white. There's a pack of bubble gum, a candy bar and a comic book on the dash. I can't help smiling. It looks like

27

Curley has a little growing up to do. I spend the next hour scouring the highway and the back roads for the green car, but it's probably in the next county by now.

You don't have to look twice to see that the Central Valley is not the California of movie stars, swimming pools and ginger-bread tans. That doesn't mean there aren't a few rich folk driving fancy cars. You just count them on one hand. Outside the feed store and local watering holes are battered pickup trucks, horse trailers and geriatric Model Ts driven by men with creased leather faces and dusty or mucky cowboy boots, depending on the season. We have the same stores and services you'll find in any small town, a right side of the tracks, a wrong side of the tracks, a crumbling Chinatown, and a Hooverville along the riverbank.

In summer the valley is a red-hot frying pan, and in winter the cold freezes the snot to your face, but it's still beautiful country that takes your breath away, with its fields of fat cattle, lion-brown hills and rocky outcroppings. In spring the valley blooms like the Garden of Eden and in autumn the season collapses with a sigh into a few short days of idyllic weather before the cold drops its relentless hammer.

Our claim to fame is growing things, and we grow them like nobody else. You name it, we grow it: grapes and olives, peaches, cherries, apples, almonds, oranges, apricots and plums. On the coast it's lettuce, berries, artichokes and Brussels sprouts. If you grow it, someone has to pick it. Before the Dust Bowl migration it was the Mexicans. Now it's dog-eat-dog: Okies, Hispanics and a few blacks escaping Jim Crow, all elbowing for a place at a table with too few plates.

Since the cold weather hit, things have been slow at the station. In the last week I've gone out on a urinating in public, use of profanity in the presence of women and children, a housewife cracking her husband on the head with a turkey platter, and a cockfight on Gonzales Road. It doesn't take a detective with 15 years in law enforcement to resolve these issues.

I drive by the levy where a group of men are filling sandbags, make one more sweep of the highway as far as the Kingsolver's apple sheds, then turn around and bounce back over the bridge into town. As I pass the auction barn, two men on ladders are hanging a banner over the door, another man on the ground shouting orders. In big red letters it reads, 'Deutschlander Social Club. Membership By Invitation Only. Lectures. Brats. Beer on tap'. I look at my watch. As soon as I hit town I pull into the Tammany Hall Bar. It's lunch time. I can use a beer myself.

*   *   *

Angel steps through the double glass doors onto the sidewalk as the first tentative drops of rain tap the canopy of her umbrella. Across the street, a light burns in the window of the Bookworm, the green-and-white awning snapping in a rising wind. She walks to the corner and crosses at the intersection of Cork and Avalon. When she exits the store with Margaret Mitchell's new novel, carefully double-bagged, the temperature has fallen and the rain comes down more steadily.

The air smells fresh and clean, the wind fluttering her scarf and tugging at her umbrella. When she reaches the corner a big O'Hara delivery truck is parked in the crosswalk, the driver wheeling a few cases of whiskey into the Leprechaun Lounge.

A man steps from the bar, takes a final drag from his cigarette and flicks the butt in the gutter, where it dies with a hiss. Something familiar in his bearing causes ice to form in the pit of Angel's stomach. She faces away from him as he walks in her direction. She squeezes her eyes shut. *Please, please, please, God, make me invisible!*

'It *is* you, isn't it?' he says with a big, friendly smile. 'It's been what, two — maybe three years?' His hair is center-parted, white-blond; his eyes ice-blue. He'd be a photographer's dream if a black splotch in the iris of his left eye didn't stand out like a horsefly on a blueberry tart.

She ignores him until she feels his leather-gloved hand on her elbow. She shrugs him away. 'Don't touch me.'

A stranger would look at this man and see wealth, education and elegant manners. Men would emulate him and women give up their virtue before noticing the unspeakable sins that crawl like tropical parasites beneath his skin. He raises an eyebrow, his smile revealing a row of straight white teeth. 'Come on, Angel. No use pretending you don't know me.'

'Please, go away. I don't want to talk to you.'

He looks surprised, perhaps a bit offended. 'Why the cold shoulder? You were a lot friendlier when you hooked for Axel Teague.'

'Not by choice,' she says, their eyes locking.

He finds that amusing. 'You were his lucky ticket back then, all blonde and delicious, like a piece of candy in gold foil.' He licks his lips and she turns away. The delivery man gets back in his truck and pulls out of the crosswalk. As Angel steps from the curb his hand closes like a vice on her upper arm, his face an inch from hers. His cologne triggers memories that return with nauseating clarity.

'Don't rush off now that we've found one another again,' he says. 'How about an encore for old times' sake?'

'That's never going to happen.'

'I bet you didn't know that Teague was into me for fifteen big ones back then. I would have put a bullet in his head if he hadn't handed you over that night. I almost believed him when he said it was your first time, but they all say that, don't they?' He laughs unpleasantly.

'I was thirteen years old. I don't know how you can live with yourself.'

'Oh, come on. It couldn't have been that bad. It was sure good for me.' He smiles to himself, remembering. 'If I could take one memory to my grave, that would be it.'

'That day cannot come soon enough to please me.'

He digs his fingers into her arm. 'You've got one sharp tongue on you, kid. You better be careful how you use it.' She tries to pull free but he only tightens his grip.

'Don't underestimate me,' she says, but

she trembles as she says it. 'I'm not that helpless little girl anymore.'

He laughs out loud and releases his grip. The light turns from green to red and there are too many cars to make a safe getaway. 'What are you, a hundred pounds? I guess I should be shaking in my shoes. Since we're on the subject, whatever happened to Teague? I haven't seen him around lately.'

'You can visit him in Oakwood Cemetery.'

'Meaning what?'

'Meaning I shot him in the throat two years ago. He tried to swallow the bullet, but he didn't have a chaser. Like you, he wouldn't take no for an answer.'

He backs off a step or two. 'You can't be serious.'

'But, I am, Mr. Dietrich. You could go to prison for what you did to me. Maybe it's not too late to put you there.'

'What did you call me?'

'It doesn't matter what phony name you used back then. You're Leland Dietrich. If you wanted to keep your identity secret, you should have kept your face off the society page. If Mrs. Dietrich doesn't know who she married, maybe it's time she found out.'

His hand shoots out and grabs her by the back of the neck, dragging her down the sidewalk toward a fancy yellow car with red leather upholstery. She struggles and cries out, but her cries are lost in the wind. She stumbles. Her book drops to the sidewalk and her umbrella somersaults down the sidewalk. With a squeal of tires, a green cab swings to the curb. It's young Tom Kelly from the cab stand, punching the horn until people in the street take notice. He's a strong-shouldered, handsome fellow with rusty auburn curls poking from beneath his driver's cap.

'Help me, Tom!' she cries, as he jumps from the cab.

After a moment's indecision, Dietrich pushes her roughly to the sidewalk. Tom helps her to her feet and retrieves her book. He pushes her safely inside the cab and slams the door shut.

Dietrich jumps behind the wheel of his car and peels away from the curb as Tom scrambles for something to write on.

Before the fancy car turns down the next side street, Tom has the license plate number written inside a matchbook cover. He puts it in his pocket and gets back behind the wheel.

'Are you okay?' he says, checking his side-view mirror and pulling into traffic.

She covers a skinned knee with her hand. 'Yes, just a bit shaken up.'

'Do you want me to call Jack?'

'No, please don't. Don't call anybody.'

'Who was that?' he asks.

'Just some drunk,' she says. 'I don't know what I would have done if you hadn't come along.'

*   *   *

Frances Dietrich watches the drama from her parked Mercedes down the block. She's dressed in jodhpurs and the raincoat she bought in London where she met Leland, a German teaching something-or-other at an English university. Frances is what's called a handsome woman, meaning forceful and unpretty. She's cut from the same durable fabric as Joan Crawford and Bette

36

Davis, both of whom she admires.

She watches Leland drive away, sets her opera glasses on the dash and thoughtfully taps a smoke from a pack of Old Golds. His secret life isn't as secret as he thinks it is. When he goes into Little Ireland or Chinatown it's not for corned beef or chop suey.

On the seat beside her, a 1910 Police Positive .38 special sits beside a silver whiskey flask, both gifts from her father on her sixteenth birthday, a time when her girlfriends were fluttering over hope chests and bridal magazines. Not Frances. She's always been a no-nonsense girl.

Fran is the only offspring of infamous bootlegger Red O'Hara. When he was shot in the back off-loading contraband liquor in Monterey Bay, she inherited his fortune, his steel backbone and his serious cigarette cough. Now that Prohibition has ended, the fleet of brown-and-yellow O'Hara trucks continues to supply every liquor store and bar in the county.

She smokes aggressively and watches the cab deposit the girl in front of the Rexford Hotel. The kid was clearly terrified when Leland accosted her, almost as if they'd crossed paths before. The cold irritates her raw lungs and triggers a coughing jag that leaves her eyes watering. When she finally catches her breath, she spits bright red blood into her pristine handkerchief. She blames the damp weather and lights a fresh cigarette off the cinder of the last.

★　★　★

'Let me help you into the lobby,' says Tom.

'No, please. I don't want to make a fuss.'

Tom walks reluctantly back to the cab stand. He wants to ask her out to dinner or a movie, but the opportunity always slips away.

Angel runs into the recessed entry, umbrella gone, a shoe damaged, but her book intact. She still has nightmares about that long-ago night with Dietrich. People can sometimes reclaim things that have been stolen from them, but the innocence of childhood isn't one of them.

A movement in the corner of the sheltered entry catches her eye. She hears a whine, and two big brown eyes look up from a pugged dog-face with big bat ears. With his serious underbite and squat body, this little fellow is ugly in the most adorable way. She slips the book inside her coat and kneels down.

'Bo, what are you doing out here? You're soaking wet.' Seventy-eight-year-old Lulu Barker doesn't go anywhere without her dog. Angel looks through the double doors and sees Albie reading a comic next to the cigarette machine. He hurries outside when Angel raps on the glass.

'What's Bo doing out here?' he asks.

'I don't know,' she says, gathering the trembling little creature in her arms. 'Let's go to my room and get him dried off.'

'Where's Lulu?'

'I don't know, but I have a feeling something is terribly wrong.'

3

When *Up To Date* comes on, Madame Zarina turns the radio to music so she doesn't have to think about the bad things going on in the world. She was born Cathleen Rose Cook, but she's Cookie to her friends. She walks to the window overlooking Cork Street as the first drops of rain begin to fall.

After her husband Skipper died, Cookie moved into the apartment above Joe Crisalli's Bakery, with its pink scalloped awning and charming bistro tables. Heavenly scents fill the entire building: cinnamon, vanilla, powdered sugar and coconut.

The first thing she did when she moved in seven years ago was hang her neon sign outside the upstairs window:

MADAME ZARINA. FORTUNES
TOLD FOR A DIME.

Although she uses an exotic name to attract customers, she doesn't wear a turban or pretend to be a gypsy princess. On any given day she's likely to give a reading in her housecoat and slippers, her grey hair fluffy with short poodle curls. When the weather allows, she can count on five or six customers a day. A few dimes here and there are nothing to sneeze at when gas is ten cents a gallon and bread eight cents a loaf.

As she stands at the window, a sharp flash of lightning blinds her and she flinches away from the pane. A vibration begins in her head and the muscles tighten painfully around her left eye. Migraine. It takes very little to wake the monster in its cave: a flash of light . . . a chemical odor . . . a sip of wine. Dr. McBane says only kidney stones or childbirth compare to the pain of migraine. Cookie doesn't need a doctor to tell her that. She washes two aspirin down and hopes she can head it off at the pass.

The headaches began when she was knocked unconscious in a buckboard accident at the age of nine, the visions following shortly thereafter. Their family priest called in an exorcist, but the ritual didn't take and the nuns at school said she had the devil in her. Her childhood doctor said she might outgrow the spells, but at 67 it was highly unlikely.

McBane calls her headaches 'aberrant episodes' because they're accompanied by dream-visions, sometimes as clear as snapshots, other times as surreal as a Salvador Dali painting.

After one of her visions a few years back she led police to the bludgeoned body of three-year-old Bucky Chapelle, hidden in a culvert on Silver Creek. Rather than gratitude, she was accused of complicity in the crime. How could she know so much if she hadn't been there? She was exonerated when Bucky's stepfather confessed to 'maybe going overboard' with his discipline when the boy dropped his cigarettes in the toilet.

Cookie became less forthcoming after that. When fourteen-year-old Gretchen Fry gave birth in secret and extinguished the child's brief flame of life, she kept her own counsel. Six months later the remains of the infant were discovered beneath the chicken coop by the family dog. Even if she'd reported the incident, the baby wouldn't have been less dead.

Then came the stabbing of Louise Crowley, a girl who'd been left to die in a remote section of the cold, rainy woods. Because she believed the girl might still be alive she risked coming forward, and her information was instrumental in saving the girl's life. Even the most skeptical cop has to admit there's something to the mysterious visions of Madame Zarina.

Joe climbs the inner staircase and Cookie invites him in. He's an industrious, handsome man, tall and fit with silver hair at the temples, and kind brown eyes and a straight, solid nose she finds very sexy. He's considered quite the catch among the growing population of local widows.

Joe looks approvingly around the cozy parlor with its over-stuffed velvet sofa and chair. A flowered rug covers the floor and gold tassels secure the soft scarlet drapes.

On a round table in the center of the room, a crystal ball rests on a cloth of midnight-blue brocade. There's a grand-father clock in the corner and Maxfield Parrish prints on the papered walls. Cookie is really quite the gal. He walks over and hands her a pink donut box.

'Your favorites,' he says. 'French twists with cherry frosting.'

'You are so naughty,' she says. 'You know I love all things French, including perfume, lace and kisses.' They share a moment of laughter and she gives him a peck on the cheek. She opens the box. 'Look at all these. You're going to make me fat.' She looks up and sees that he's wearing his top coat. 'Don't tell me you're closing early.'

'It's the storm, Cookie. I'm going home to make sure Cooley delivered my sandbags. The Saddle Shop closed an hour ago because nobody knows how bad it's going to get. Why don't you come home with me? I hate leaving you by yourself.'

'I don't think so, Joe. If the creek goes over I'll be stranded out there. Besides, the weatherman says it might not get as bad as predicted.' It's really about her headache, but Joe already has enough on his plate.

'You shouldn't be living alone anymore, Cookie, especially with your heart condition,' he says.

'It's just a little irregularity, Joe. That's what the pills are for.'

He studies her face. A beat or two passes in silence and she knows what's coming. 'What?' she says, taking a bite of donut. 'Do I have frosting on my nose?'

'What about my proposal, Cookie? I hope you've given it some serious consideration this time.'

'Believe me, Joe, I'm thinking as fast as I can, but what's wrong with things the way they are?'

'Cookie, I'm lonely in that big house. Sometimes I wake up at night and feel like the last person on the planet. No one to put my arms around. No one to talk with. You've had five years to think.'

'You do have Pumpkin,' she says, with a bewildered look.

'Yes, a cat is very nice, but he doesn't

keep up his end of the conversation.'

'I don't mean to be so stubborn. You know how I feel about you, but after Skip died, I swore I'd never get trapped like that again. I wasted so many years putting up with that cad.'

'You were young, Cookie. You made a mistake. Besides, I'm not Skip.'

She laughs and rolls her eyes. 'Skip wasn't Skip either until I married him! Then I found out who he *really* was.' Her head begins to throb just thinking about her disastrous marriage.

'All right, you win.' Joe throws his hands up in surrender. 'The armory is opening its doors in case it floods, but you can't wait until the last minute. If you like, I can drive you over.'

Cookie bristles. 'With all the Shanty Irish piling in from across the tracks? I'd rather be hit by lightning.'

'You are one stubborn woman,' he says, patting her shoulder. Then more seriously: 'I know a lot of ladies who'd give anything if just one person cared if they lived or died.'

'I'll call if I need you.'

'Not tonight,' he says, a cool note of resignation creeping into his voice. 'At least I know where I stand.'

'Now Joe, don't . . . '

He turns abruptly and goes back down the stairs.

★ ★ ★

As Joe warms up the car he looks up at Cookie's apartment, where a ruby lamp glows behind the pane. She's been part of his life since they played kick-the-can as kids. He was despondent when she eloped with that handsome rascal, Skip Millstone. Skip probably broke her heart a million times with his philandering ways, people pitying her and laughing behind her back. A year later Joe caved in to parental pressure and married Mildred Lovisoni. He never made her feel second-best, although the torch he carried for Cookie continued to flicker in secret.

Seven years ago Skip was killed behind the wheel of his roadster, a foot on the gas and his eye on a pretty young thing swinging a tennis racket. Pow! Right into a tree. Joe figured he had it coming.

Cookie reclaimed her maiden name, something unheard of in her generation. She said that Millstone was a bit weighty and she couldn't lug it around anymore. The judge laughed and granted her request. A few months later, Mildred lost her struggle with lupus, and after a reasonable period of mourning, he set his cap once again, for Cookie.

After all these years she still fascinates him. He'd asked her once if she could really tell fortunes, if she could see into the future when she gazed into her crystal ball. Her response was surprisingly candid. She told him the ball was merely the focal point of her intuitive energies. Her talent was reading people, analyzing their concerns and knowing what kind of advice they needed to hear. It usually involved romance, money or guilt. How complicated was that? In the process, she'd become privy to more sins and secrets than Father Doyle at St. Finnbar's or Chief Garvey down at the station. People are more inclined to confide in someone who lacks the power to relegate them to hell or jail. As for the visions? They're the real McCoy, beyond her understanding or control.

Rain taps on the roof of the car and Joe turns on the windshield wipers. He pulls into the street and heads toward home, where his fat orange cat waits in the window. He's not getting any younger and he's tired of lying alone in bed listening to the clock tick away the hours.

Something's got to give and it looks like Cookie isn't going to budge.

★ ★ ★

I head home as soon as Angel calls the station and tells me that Lulu is unaccounted for. Jake is unlocking the Barkers' room with a passkey when I arrive. We hear a moan and Angel, Jake and I rush to the bedroom where Lulu's husband Roland is cussing up a storm. Weighed down by a heavy plaster body cast, he's wedged awkwardly between his bed and the wall, with Lulu nowhere in sight.

'I pounded on that blasted wall half the night before I realized 307 was vacant,' says Roland. He's a big man who stumbled off the curb four weeks ago, broke his femur and cracked his pelvis. Now he's 275 lbs. of dead weight.

I look at Jake. He looks at me. He's a tall colored man with shoulders like a bison. 'Okay, let's do it,' he says. He takes Roland's upper body and motions for me to take his legs. One, two, three, and we hoist him onto the bed, the patient grumbling all the way. My bad leg makes a popping sound at the hip and I pretend not to notice the pain that shoots down the sciatic nerve into my big toe. Angel fluffs his pillow and gently tucks the blankets around him.

'Are you comfortable now, Mr. Barker?' she asks.

'Do I look comfortable, missy?' Angel turns her head and bites her lip to keep from smiling.

'Where is Lulu?' I ask. 'Angel found Bo in the rain.'

'Oh, you mean the crazy woman I live with? She took off during the night. I tried to stop her and look where I ended up. She's not herself anymore. Yesterday she looks at me and says, 'Don't I know you from someplace?' How do I respond to something like that?'

'Any idea where she's gone?'

'The all-night café. Maybe the park. She forgot her purse so at least she's not out there blowing my money.'

'We certainly can't have that,' I say. I turn to Jake. 'I'm going to drive around the neighborhood. If I don't find her in thirty minutes or so, I'm filing a missing persons.' I turn back to Roland. 'What is she wearing?'

'My raccoon coat, bobby socks and tennis shoes with holes in the toes.'

Albie appears in the doorway with Bo wrapped in a towel. He wiggles free and runs to the bedside, whining and prancing and waiting to be lifted onto the bed.

'Get him away from me!' says Roland. 'Nothing smells worse than a damp dog. Lock him in the bathroom.'

'I'll hold him,' says Albie, picking him up.

'Hold him? You can keep him.'

'Can I really, Mr. Roland?'

'French bulldogs are the most useless creatures on earth. That's why Lulu's sister gave him to us. They can't hunt or herd. They can't breed without assistance or give birth without veterinary intervention. If they try to swim, their big heads pull them right to the bottom faster than the *Titanic*.'

Albie walks to the window overlooking the back alley, Bo nibbling affectionately at his chin. 'I think you're cute,' he says, and gives him a squeeze. Beyond the window the rain falls steadily, the power lines whipping between the poles. 'Where's your car, Mr. Roland?'

'Where it always is, parked next to the garbage cans.'

'Ain't there now.'

'You blind? It's the green Chevy sedan.'

Green sedan. That gets my antennae quivering.

'Like I say, it just ain't there,' says the boy.

'Where do you keep the keys, Mr. Barker?' I ask.

52

'In the ashtray by the phone.'

I walk over and take a look. 'They're gone.'

'Since when has Lulu started driving?' asks Jake.

'She doesn't drive,' says Roland. 'I gave her lessons once, but it was like teaching a monkey to balance a checkbook. She couldn't tell the difference between the gas and the brake no matter how many times I explained it. You need to get cracking, Jack. I want my car back in one piece.'

Jake turns to Albie. 'Go get Agnes Peel. She'll be cleaning on the second floor. Tell her to bring Mr. Barker some soup. Then I'm calling his doctor.'

'And tell her not to forget the crackers.' says Roland. 'I can't eat soup without crackers. Not the big ones, either. Those little round ones.'

I can only take Roland Barker in small doses. 'I have to go,' I say.

'I'll ride down with you,' says Angel. 'Hank is holding my new book at the desk.' As we ride the elevator to the lobby I notice how pale she is. 'Mr. Barker is the most ungrateful man I've ever met,' she says. 'I don't know how Lulu tolerates him.'

'By getting dementia.'

'Oh Jack, you're terrible.'

'I know I am. Did you know there's a button missing from your coat?'

Angel looks down. 'So there is. It's probably somewhere in the room.'

'Are you all right? You're not coming down with something, are you?'

'I got cold coming back from the book store. I didn't think the light would ever change.'

The elevator bounces to a stop in the lobby and we get out. Hank retrieves her book from behind the desk and she thanks him. I peel a few bucks from my wallet. 'Here, in case you need something. Promise me you'll eat.'

'I promise.'

I tuck a stray lock of hair behind her ear. It's damp with rain and her hands are like ice. Something's not right, something more than the weather, but I can't put my finger on it.

* * *

In a house set back from the highway, Kenny Geiger, age 6, sits at the table with his chin in his hands, looking at the empty chair across from him. The wind is up and a shingle flies past the kitchen window. His mother looks up from a sink of sudsy water. 'Kenny dear, you might as well finish the last pork chop. If Georgie was coming, he'd be here by now.'

'I can't, Mom. I'm stuffed.'

'I can,' says Mr. Geiger, balancing his cigar stub on the edge of his plate. He picks up his fork, but his heroic girth seriously impedes his reach. Kay seizes the moment and stabs the chop with a fork. Within seconds she has it wrapped in waxed paper and in the ice box, obviously quite pleased with herself. She has a friendly, mischievous face and a head of frizzy Orphan Annie curls. She's as fit and quick as Harry is fat and slow.

'What the..?'

'I'm saving you from yourself, Harry. You're beginning to look like William Howard Taft.'

'Then maybe I'll run for president.'

'You can't even run to the mailbox.'

Kenny snickers.

'You're a wicked woman,' says Harry, unable to suppress a smile. 'A wicked, wicked woman.' She walks behind his chair and playfully musses his hair.

Harry and Kenny push away from the table as Kay washes and dries the last of the dishes. Harry thumps into his broken-down easy chair and picks up *The Saturday Evening Post*. Kenny goes to the front window and looks into the fading daylight. Kay comes up behind him.

'I wish you wouldn't worry so much, Kenny. When Georgie saw the rain coming he probably went home to be with his family.'

'Mom, you don't understand. He was right behind me. When I turned around he was gone. All he talked about was the sleepover. His family's been eating cold beans from the can, and he knew you were making pork chops.'

'I'm sure he'll tell you all about it on Monday.'

'That Allen kid could use a few extra pounds,' says Harry.

'You could give him a few of yours, dear.'

'Very funny. Besides, I'm not so sure I want him sleeping on our sheets, and don't pretend you don't know what I'm talking about.'

'It's not a crime to be poor, Harry.'

He raises his arms in a helpless gesture. 'Don't come down on *me*. I didn't make him that way.'

'You're talking about my best friend,' says Kenny.

'Which puzzles me no end,' says Harry, shaking his head.

'Can't we change the subject to something pleasant?' says Kay.

'Sure.' Harry closes his magazine and rubs his growling stomach. 'Everybody at work is talking about the Mulholland Dam collapse of '28. Destroyed the whole town of Castaic. Every living thing. Now, *there's* a history lesson I bet they don't teach you in school.'

'Is that going to happen to us?' says Kenny, turning from the window.

'Of course not,' says Kay. 'Even if the levy gives it could never be that bad.'

'Yup, the whole town gone,' says Harry. 'Every baby in its crib. Every chicken and mule.'

'Must you go on like that in front of the boy? You'll give him nightmares.'

'Over six hundred people died in that flood,' he continues, undeterred. 'They never even counted the wetbacks camped below the dam, so it's probably closer to two thousand.'

'Thanks for cheering us up, Harry,' says Kay. 'I don't know what we'd do without you. Get into your pyjamas, Kenny, and we'll read a while.'

4

I walk down the sidewalk past the magazine stand at the end of the day, mist blowing between the buildings like spray flung from a wave. The pink-and-purple neon from the theater ripples in the gutter like fingerpaint.

'Officer Dunning!' Tom Kelly pays the vendor for his hot dog and walks my way. He's outgoing and good-natured with a handsome, honest face beneath his chauffeur's cap.

'Yes, Tom. How you doing?'

'Fine, sir. My dad's moving on in years, so he's turned the business over to me. We've gone from one cab to three in under a year.'

'That's great, Tom. Congratulations.'

Tom reaches in his pocket and hands me a matchbook. 'Look under the cover,' he says. I flip it open and see a license plate number scribbled in pencil.

'Someone giving you trouble?' I ask.

'No, sir. This is about your daughter.'

'My daugh — '

'Miss Angel,' he says.

My tongue won't move and Tom keeps talking. 'A man in this fancy yellow car tried to . . . well . . . he tried to kidnap her. I couldn't believe it was really happening. I swear, if I hadn't been driving by, I don't know what would have happened.'

'Kidnap her? Are you sure?' I say, putting the matchbook in my pocket.

'He came out of the Leprechaun Lounge and grabbed her. When I pulled up he was trying to force her into his car.'

'Is she all right?'

'Roughed up a bit, but she wouldn't let me call you. I hope I'm doing the right thing by going against her wishes.' The button. Her cold hands. Things were beginning to make sense.

'Thank you, Tom. Are you all right?'

'Sure, I'm fine, sir.'

'What time did this happen?'

'Just after noon. She was coming from the bookstore, minding her own business.'

That would have been *before* I'd come

home to check on the Barkers. 'What did this guy look like?'

'An evil movie star.'

'I don't know what that means.'

'The handsome guy you think is a hero, then halfway through the movie you know he's the one who did it — who did the murder.'

'Okay, I think I get it. I'll run the plate by the chief and see who the car belongs to.' Tom stands there like he has more to say. 'Anything else?' I ask.

Tom clears his throat. 'Do you think Angel would like to go to the movies with me sometime? It's right across the street and I'd have her home early.'

I look at my watch.

'Can we talk another time, Tom? I have to run.'

I ride the elevator to the second floor, a tightness in my chest making it hard to breathe. 'Your daughter', he'd said. *She's not my daughter, she's my . . . my what? Tom held a mirror to my face that I'm afraid to look into. I can think of a million reasons I want Angel and a million reasons she'd be better off with someone*

61

*else . . . someone like Tom Kelly
. . . sober . . . honest . . . a young man
going places in this world.*

Angel sits in the easy chair, reading.
She smiles when I walk in the door, her
hair a golden tangle in the circle of
lamplight. 'Have they found Lulu?' she
asks, looking up from her book.

'Not yet. The boys are still looking.'

'I hate to think of her out there in this
weather,' she says, setting her book on the
lamp table.

'Me too. At least she has the raccoon
coat.' I glance at the book. *Gone with the
Wind*. 'How is it?'

'It's great, but when I started reading
to Albie, he got the giggles and went to
play with Bo.'

'Read him James Oliver Curwood. He
writes adventure stories.'

'I'm still furious with that teacher at
Orchard School, the one who wouldn't let
Albie enroll. I know why and so do you.'

'I'd forget it. Father Doyle has him on
the waiting list at St. Finnbar's. He's a
smart kid. He'll get a good education.'

Angel laughs. 'You told me you hated

Catholic School.'

'I did, but I'm the only guy in the department who can conjugate Latin verbs.'

'Sounds terribly romantic.'

Most evenings we sit by the window and look out at the lights. Tonight the curtains are closed. I wait for her to tell me what happened today, but she doesn't and I don't press.

'Albie is crazy about Bo,' she says. 'You know that Lulu will want him back.'

'I know.' I pour two B and Bs, put one on the lamp table and take the chair across from hers. 'You know you can tell me anything, don't you, Angel?'

She looks at me a long moment before she speaks. 'You've always been there for me, Jack. I've never doubted that.'

★   ★   ★

Night. Rain swirls beyond the window and Cookie's migraine hits like a hammer. Rain surfs past the window and the neon sign beneath the window swings in the wind. When the pain becomes

63

unbearable she goes for her elixir.

'This should do the trick,' Dr. McBane had told her when he handed her the bottle of golden liquid. 'We've tried all the conventional remedies and nothing has helped, but you must understand, if anyone asks, it didn't come from me.'

One evening she and Joe were having dinner in Chinatown when they saw McBane exit the back door of Li Dock Qwan's Apothecary. He hurried to his car with a small bundle in his hand, head down, hat pulled low.

'It's no secret anymore,' said Joe.

'I didn't see a thing,' said Cookie stubbornly.

'It's illegal, or he wouldn't have to sneak around like that.'

'Eat your eggroll and mind your own business.'

Now Cookie wishes she'd gone with Joe. She can't blame him for being angry, the way she's kept him dangling. Maybe it's time to say 'yes' before Ginger Everly moves in on her territory. She's seen the way the librarian looks at him when he checked out books, even when Cookie is standing there big as life.

Pushing aside the veils that drape her canopy bed, Cookie slips under the covers and swallows two thimbles of elixir. It's sweet, with the bitter under-taste of burned tangerines. She's been warned not to exceed the recommended dosage, but there have been times the pain makes it hard to think straight.

She barely has time to tuck into her pillow before she sinks into somnolent darkness, the whisper of blood in her ears like the gentle rush of the sea. Down, down, down into the black abyss. As her mortal eyes close, her inner eye opens like the lens of a camera and a dreamscape comes into focus:

Cookie finds herself standing across the highway from Orchard School, the one-room schoolhouse. For the moment, her headache is relegated to another dimension of time and space. The teacher watches the children scatter after class lets out. It's not her old friend, Nellie Brown, but a new scrubbed-faced young teacher with a cameo brooch at her throat. She waltzes in circles, holding a black lunchbox like a dancing partner. Her maidenly bun loosens and her hair flies free. Wind balloons her long dark skirt, revealing a red silk petticoat. A car with a broken tailpipe sparks along the pavement, sending the children laughing and shrieking into the orchard next to the playground. The teacher . . .

There's a deafening crash and Cookie's eyes pop open as the clock strikes three. She stares into the darkness of her bedroom, her headache returning with a roar. Something dreadful has happened on the street outside, and being ripped from sleep so suddenly has sent her heart thumping erratically. She places a nitro-glycerin pill under her tongue, spilling a few tablets on the bedspread.

A pickup truck and a black Hudson have collided at the intersection. It's a chaotic scene of blowing rain, twisted metal and shattered glass. A man stumbles from the Hudson and collapses at the curb. The other driver is slumped over the steering wheel. Cookie makes her way to the living room phone and calls for an ambulance.

The pain in her head is blinding. She stumbles back to the bedroom and empties her bottle of elixir. There wasn't much left anyway, was there? Only one step to the bed, but she doesn't make it. Her knees buckle and she strikes her head on the nightstand on the way to the floor.

5

The sound of a chainsaw dominates Joe's dream. He stands in a redwood forest with trees toppling around him. A big one with a trunk the size of a caboose comes right at him. He yelps and wakes with a jolt, rain tapping the windowpane, a car revving its engine in the road outside the house.

The luminous dial on the clock reads 2:00 a.m. He pulls the blankets over his head. *Rev, rev, rev! Grind, grind, grind!* No doubt some idiot heading home from the bar has bottomed out in the ditch. Pumpkin climbs on his pillow and begins grooming. *Scratch, chew, rev, grind!* For heaven's sake, can't a decent person get any rest around here?

Grumbling under his breath, he shoves his bare feet into rubber boots and slips a raincoat over his pyjamas. As he picks up his flashlight and heads for the stairs, Pumpkin curls into a fluffy knot on his

68

pillow. He grabs his fishing hat on the way out the door and squishes through the wet grass. He walks across the narrow unpaved lane and jerks the car door open.

'For god's sake, turn the engine off before you strip the gears.' Between his frustration with Cookie and having his sleep disrupted, he's in an uncharacteristically ornery mood. An unseen hand switches off the engine. 'Now, turn off the lights or you'll drain the battery.' The lights go off. 'What's wrong with you? Are you an imbecile?'

'No, señor.' A shapely leg in a high-heeled shoe emerges from the car. A shapely body follows the shapely leg. The young lady's not very tall, but she has more treacherous curves than the rollercoaster on the Santa Cruz Beach Boardwalk. Her curly black hair is stacked high on her head, her earrings glittering like chandeliers from a fancy hotel. She straightens her dress, a racy pink number, snug at the waist and hips, then flaring to the knee in a series of flouncy ruffles. 'I am so sorry to bother you, señor. I am an excellent driver, but

69

these little foreign cars have a mind of their own, no?'

'No . . . I mean . . . yes, yes of course.' Instead of chewing her out he's telling her it's no trouble, no trouble at all; that foreign cars are certainly more stubborn than domestic models.

'I am Chita Montoya.' To his surprise, she's alert and quite sober.

'Joe Crisalli,' he says.

'Please to meet you, Cho.'

He bends over and sees a guitar, a pair of silver candlesticks, a gun case and a jewelry box in the back seat. 'What's all this stuff?' he says.

'I'm just move today to Santa Paulina and I'm not so sure where I got off track. I think maybe map upside-down. I've come teach at Top Hat School of Dance. Is famous. You've heard of it, no?'

'I'm afraid not. I go to the senior dances at the church with . . . you know . . . the single dances.' He was about to say 'with Cookie', but some invisible force stopped him.

'Single dances? I can no believe a handsome man like you is no married.'

'I was for many years, but she passed away,' he says.

'Can I use your phone to call a cab? I can have a tow truck out here in the morning.'

One tire hangs over the ditch and Joe could easily pull her car onto the road with his pickup, but . . . 'All right, come inside before the rain ruins your dress.'

'You are *muy simpatico*, señor.' She grabs her purse and trots after him to the house.

Three cups of hot chocolate later and they're still waiting for the cab. Chita is pleasant company, vivacious and talkative, but Joe is running out of small talk. There's only so much one can say about baking bread and frosting cupcakes.

'You have a lovely house,' she says. 'Is *muy bonita*.'

'Would you like the guided tour?' He hadn't planned to show her the house, but she'd somehow weaseled it out of him.

'Oh, *si*. Someday I will have a house of my own, but first I must work very hard.' Walking past the fireplace in the living room, Chita sees a blue-and-white Chinese urn on the mantelpiece. 'A ginger jar, no?'

'My wife's ashes. I was to have scattered them, but the time was never right.'

'When did she pass, Cho?'

'Six or seven years back. It's been a while.'

'No wonder you no married. What woman wants to share husband with ashes of dead wife?'

'I'd never thought of it that way.'

'Besides, is dark inside jar. Scatter ashes into the light.'

'I'll think it over.'

'No more thinking. Chust time to do.'

The stairs to the second floor are narrow and steep. Chita turns an ankle and stumbles against him and Joe feels body heat radiating off her skin. The way she looks at him fills him with unease. Her perfume is dark and intoxicating, like the kind of flowers that open after midnight. Joe is a bit short of breath as they continue up the stairs.

'This is my room,' he says. 'I like solid

furniture, no frills and no nicknacks.' She fusses over Pumpkin and they move on to the guestroom with its patch quilt, rocking chair and hooked rug.

'Is big house for one person, no? You could get roommate, make extra money.'

'I don't think so.' They continue down the hall. He'd intended to go back downstairs, but Chita steps inside his wife's old room and snaps on the overhead light.

'Your wife had her own room?'

'She wasn't well. My snoring bothered her.'

The furniture is white French provincial, Mildred's portrait above the bed revealing an average-looking woman with a high opinion of herself. Her clothes are still in the closet, perfume bottles and a monogrammed silver comb and brush on the vanity. Chita picks up the brush. 'M,' she says. 'M for Montoya.'

'I don't think so. Her name was Mildred.' He takes the brush from her hand and returns it to its proper place. 'Let's go down,' he says. 'It's too warm up here.' Chita reaches out and takes his hand. A little quiver runs up his arm. Car

73

lights sweep across the window. A car horn sounds. 'Good lord,' he says, reclaiming his hand. 'He'll wake up the whole neighborhood.'

'My cab. I go now.'

At the front door Chita thanks him for his hospitality, then takes a business card from her purse and scribbles something on the reverse side. 'Is for complimentary dance lesson. Tomorrow night. Eight o'clock. You soon be tango like Rudolph Valentino.'

'Oh, I really don't think . . . ' He tries to keep his eyes on her face, but they drift to the bodice of her dress. She stands on tiptoe and kisses him lightly on the mouth, brushing against him sort-of accidentally on purpose. Her eyes are dark and sparkling, her lips the color of deep red wine.

'Be honest, Cho. I know when a man is die to play with fire. Eight o'clock. You no come, I cry like baby.'

6

Leland Dietrich waits for the clock in the foyer to strike two, then seeing no light beneath Frances's bedroom door, coasts his yellow bomb down the driveway. At the bottom of the hill, beyond earshot of the house, he fires up the engine. He streaks through town, over the railroad track, beyond the packing house and into Chinatown. He parks near the Dragon Gate, then ventures on foot into the hutongs . . . the narrow alleys no wider than a man's arm span.

He walks through passageways smelling of garbage, urine and incense. Buildings list and crumble, each rickety floor tacked above the shaky level beneath. Bright paper lanterns are strung from balcony to balcony. Over the decades Chinatown has been destroyed by quake and arson, the inhabitants decimated by angry mobs, cholera and the Chinese Exclusion Act of 1872; but each time, it rises like a phoenix from the ashes.

Dietrich passes the silk shop, the apothecary and an opium den that sends clouds of sweet smoke into the night. Behind a grocery store window he sees shriveled black mushrooms as big as a man's fist, bouquets of dried herbs, two live geese in a wire cage, a pan of frog legs and a dozen smoked cats hanging from their hind legs like laundry on a line.

At the end of the alley, he turns sideways and squeezes through an opening between two buildings into a circular cobblestone courtyard. This is the dark heart of Chinatown. Sing-Song girls, indentured to years of slavery, beckon from barred cages containing a candle, a cot and a wash basin. The music from their lips is of carnal invitation and infinite melancholy.

Black-clad men with long braids down their backs recognize the fair-haired man who enters their world. They exchange disapproving glances as he pushes to the front of the line. Shu Ling reaches through the bars of her cage and tugs at his sleeve, but he ignores her. She used to be his favorite pleasure girl when she worked out of the master's house, but at fifteen she's used up and no longer of interest to him. He claps his leather-gloved hands and calls for Fu Gang, the richest man in Chinatown.

A coolie trots across the square to a red-pillared house with gilded cornices. Within moments the fat slave-monger appears with an obsequious bow. Fu Gang detests the arrogant foreigner, but he likes his money and would like to have more of it. In the entry a servant takes his coat and gloves and he enters a parlor decorated with ornaments of ivory and gold, carved dragon chairs and painted screens embedded with semi-precious stones. The family has done well in their chosen profession.

A young girl pours tea for an old woman who studies Dietrich over her opium pipe. The girl wears the cropped hair of childhood and teeters gracefully on tiny velvet-slippered feet, her eyes cast downcast.

'What's her name?' asks Dietrich.

'That's my mother.'

'The other one.'

'Dong Lan.'

'And its meaning?'

'Winter Orchid.'

'Winter Orchid. I like that. It has such a cool, chaste ring.'

'She's my youngest daughter and she's not for sale.'

Dietrich cuts his eyes to Fu Gang's face. 'Everything is for sale if the price is right. You told me that yourself.'

The girl's grandmother waves a hand to silence her son. Her wrinkled fingers are ringed in lapis lazuli and carnelian and in her eye is the unmistakable glitter of greed. 'This child is worth an emperor's ransom,' she says. 'Look at the nice man, Dong Lan.' The girl looks up. Her eyes are a startling emerald-green set in white porcelain features — not the first child he's seen of Irish-Chinese ancestry . . . but the loveliest.

As soon as Fu Gang opens his mouth to speak, the old woman barks at him, 'Don't be a fool! She is only a female child.' She smiles and demands American money, double the usual rate, and he agrees without hesitation. 'You may have the Cherry Blossom Room at the top of the house,' she says. Dietrich smirks as Fu Gang bows his head and silently withdraws.

A Chinese eunuch with painted lips, a flower behind his ear and a dagger in his sash appears from behind a drape and carries Dong Lan up the stairs. Before Dietrich takes a second step the withered hag holds out her hand. 'The money first.' He hands it over. When you have a rich wife, money comes easily, like water from a spigot. Their hands touch, hers cold and reptilian. When he jerks away, her laughter sounds like the crackle of dry parchment.

The upstairs hall is sweet with incense, the silvery sound of wind chimes floating up from the garden. He takes a deep breath and opens the first door on the right. The bed is big and satiny and strewn with gold-embroidered pillows. It is also empty.

Instead of the girl, he finds himself looking down the barrel of Fu Gang's gun. The eunuch jumps from behind the door and his curved dagger slices through Dietrich's shirt, leaving a long, red scratch on his soft white gut. He flees down the hall with a bullet whistling past his ear.

Dietrich is on the ground floor before he takes his next breath. Winter Orchid is gone and so is his money. He bolts from the house, a second bullet whining over his head. He hears the uproarious laughter of the men lined up at the cribs and squeezes back between the buildings into the hutong.

After a quarter mile Dietrich stumbles to a stop. If anyone in the Fatherland had dared laugh at him, he'd have cut them down with impunity. He leans against the wall of a grand house to catch his breath. Visible through the window he sees fringed red and gold lanterns hanging from the ceiling, laughter and music drifting into the street.

A slice of light spills into the alleyway and a willowy young courtesan passes through a beaded curtain. She's a painted doll with glittering ornaments in her hair. She smiles sweetly and in a tongue that needs no translation, invites him inside. Dietrich, still burning with shame and humiliation, lets out a guttural bellow. He punches the girl in the face as hard as he'd hit a man and runs wailing into the night.

*　　*　　*

In the hour before dawn, the phone rings at Frances Dietrich's bedside. 'What?' she says, snapping on the bedside lamp.

'It's Darrell Singleton, ma'am, from the Pinkerton Agency. You asked me to call as soon as I had something to report.'

'Yes, yes, go on.'

'Tonight I followed Mr. Dietrich into Chinatown. I hung back as he entered the courtyard of the Sing-Song girls. When he left, half an hour later, he was being fired at.'

Frances pulls herself up on her pillows and grabs her cigarettes. 'As in gunfire?'

'Yes. It appears he's worn out his welcome in the hutongs.'

'Will I have the pleasure of wearing widow's weeds?' she asks, coughing a light mist of blood onto the bedspread.

'Not this time, but I'm afraid his carnal

indiscretions are only the tip of the iceberg.'

'What is that supposed to mean?'

'When you met him on your grand tour, you said he was a German guest lecturer at the university.'

'Yes, he was quite cosmopolitan — educated at Oxford, spoke the Queen's English like a native Londoner.'

'Which makes him all the more dangerous, Mrs. Dietrich. According to our research he was dispatched to England to spread anti-Semitic propaganda.'

'How can you know that?'

'The documents in my report have been checked and rechecked. There's talk in Europe that the Nazis are gearing up for another war.'

'Oh, good grief! I thought we'd already had The War To End All Wars.'

'There's one more thing you need to know. The man you married was born Ludwig Gerhard von Buchholz. Usually people who change their names have something to hide.'

'Now you're stretching my credibility.'

'I deal only with the facts. His father

Heinz holds a high position in the SS.'

'Oh, come now, you can't mean he's one of those Nazi clowns who struts around with a riding crop and a Doberman Pinscher at his heels.'

'The Schutzstaffel. They're men of enormous influence. Let me remind you, an apple doesn't fall far from the tree.'

'That's all very intriguing. I'd be crushed if I hadn't ceased loving Leland ages ago. I wonder why he was so eager to come to America?'

'Your money may have been a motivating factor.'

'Daddy told me when I was just a girl that any man I married would be proposing to my money. I wasn't much of a looker and I can't say I much cared. I bet Red's up there laughing his butt off.'

'Now that his infidelities are well-documented, shall I send you a closing bill?'

'No. Keep digging. This is getting interesting.'

'By the way, Mrs. Dietrich, he's just now pulling onto your street. I'll be in touch.'

7

Saguaro Correctional
Early May 1936

Penelope Hanover makes sure the lights are out in Hedy's cabin. In the distance, the Alamillo Escarpment is dark and foreboding, coyotes yipping from the summit of the pinnacles. She fingers the cameo brooch at the throat of her blouse. For a girl who follows the rules, she's made a decision that could get her in big trouble. On the other hand, if she unravels the mystery of the missing girls, she'll be a hero. She slips quietly outside, carrying her flashlight and key ring, locking the door behind her. She picks her way over the stony ground to the administration building.

The janitorial staff have arrived, their truck parked outside the main entrance. She enters the double doors and sees no one in the hall, just a broom and floor buffer against the wall, the crew busy on the second floor. She hurries to the records room, closes the door and snaps on the desk lamp.

Patty Gregson. Velma Becker. Sarah Levin. Once she heard the names spoken into the shortwave she couldn't get them out of her head. She's convinced that something other than their disappearances links the three girls. They're listed as runaways, but she doesn't think it's that simple.

Penny sets her key ring and flashlight on the desk. In the top drawer is the key that opens the metal filing cabinet. She pulls the girls' charts and takes a seat at the desk. She starts with Patty Gregson and flips through the text. Age thirteen. Grade seven. After giving birth to Patty's little sister, Patty's mother kept repeating, 'Thank God I finally have a perfect child.' Feeling worthless and rejected, Patty smothered the baby in retaliation. She attempted suicide twice before confessing to the crime. After counseling at Saguaro, she'd become less self-destructive and her grades went from straight Fs to Ds and

Cs. Penny studies the snapshot in Patty's file. Patty is a waif with limp blonde hair and a purple birthmark that covers the entire right side of her face. Not the child her mother felt she deserved.

Penny sets the file aside and opens Velma Becker's chart. Age fifteen, grade nine, smashed the statue of St. Bernadette and poured bleach in the grotto, killing the goldfish at St. Sebastian's Church in Dry Rock. She accused Father Jerome of seducing her and her mother of aborting her when she became pregnant with his child. Both the priest and mother vehemently denied the accusations. Since her incarceration, Velma has developed a violent stammer and finally stopped talking entirely. Her photo reveals a bitter, smoldering fury . . . the look of a child betrayed.

Next is Sarah Levin, the only girl with whom Penny is acquainted. Sarah is endowed with Biblical beauty: deep brown eyes, shiny black hair and a golden-olive complexion. When Sarah's mother died, she left Sarah a college fund. When her father remarried, his new wife purchased a sable coat, draining the account. Sarah sent the fancy fur through the wash cycle of the Maytag and squeezed it through the ringer. The girl was a straight-A student and only had a month to go before release from Saguaro. Why run away with only 30 days to go? It makes no sense.

The three girls are different from one another in age, grade and offense, yet they vanished at the same time. Before that night it's doubtful they came closer to one another than passing in the hall. Mrs. Coleman, the dorm matron, said they never made it to roll call on the night they went missing. It was assumed they were hiding on the grounds, then fled under cover of darkness. Penny doubts that scenario.

She examines each file one more time, squinting at photos, rereading the text. She closes her eyes and concentrates. Patty had a birthmark, Velma a stutter. That's a vague connection, but only between the two. Sarah has neither disfigurement nor disability.

Blut. Reinheit. Mangel.

The words spin inside her head.

Blood. Purity. Defect.

Penny lets out a gasp and tosses the files back in the cabinet. She turns off the lamp, drops her flashlight and retrieves it. When she rises, her heel catches her hem and rips her skirt. Suddenly, everything makes sense and a frightening, almost incomprehensible theory takes shape.

The housekeeping staff start down the stairs to the clatter of buckets and mops. Penny snaps off the light, bolts down the hall and out the door. It isn't until she's outside that she realizes she's left her key ring behind and the key to the unlocked filing cabinet is still in her hand.

★   ★   ★

Hedy Greiss watches Penelope hurry from the building. The girl has a dangerous condition known as 'insatiable curiosity'. The accountant steps from the shadows as the housekeeping staff arrive in the lobby.

'Jesus,' she says. The head janitor turns her way.

'*Si*, señorita?'

'I just saw a woman flee the building.'

'You're the only one I see tonight, Señorita Greiss.'

'I distinctly saw Miss Hanover leave the records room.'

'At this time of night?'

'That's what concerns me. I'd better make sure everything's in order. From now on, lock the doors when your crew is at work.'

'What about you?

'You needn't worry, Jesus. I have my own key.'

Hedy snaps on the overhead in the records room. The filing cabinet is closed, but not locked. Even if Penny looked at the files, she wouldn't know what to look for. Then again, it's a chance Hedy isn't willing to take. On the desktop is a metal ring with Hanover's car key and the key to Bungalow 5. How considerate of the little idiot to leave her calling card at the scene of the crime. Now she's locked out of her cabin *and* her car.

Hedy goes through the drawers of the desk, not sure what she's looking for. She finds a jar holding petty cash. There's about twenty dollars in bills and a handful of change. She pockets the bills, hides the jar inside her coat and returns to the lobby.

'I'm afraid we have a thief in our midst,' she says, dangling Penny's keys from her fingers. 'Now the petty cash is missing.'

'You want I should wake up Mr. Churchwell?'

'I'll take care of it, Jesus. You may, however, be asked to sign a witness statement.'

8

Five days out of Oklahoma and Ed Thompson pulls the flatbed next to a ditch outside Santa Paulina. If the truck holds up, they'll turn west at Manteca, go through the Altamont Pass and on to Castroville to work the winter crops.

Ed's wife Anna and his three daughters climb stiffly from the back of the truck while Ed and his son Frankie raise the hood. The engine snaps and pings in the stillness. Frankie wraps his hand in a mechanic's rag and carefully works the radiator cap, releasing a rush of angry steam.

The girls double over in breathless laughter as their terrier, Speedy, gives the one-legged salute to every roadside weed. Anna smiles behind the Bible that seldom leaves her hand. The dog bounds down the side of the ditch, lapping and splashing in the few inches of water at the bottom. Within minutes he's worked his way thirty feet down the highway.

Father and son light their corncob pipes and give the truck a rest, the radiator hissing at their backs. They talk quietly and study the map, the breeze blowing cinders from the bowls of their pipes. They smoke in comfortable silence while the engine cools, then tap their pipes clean. Ed tops off the radiator from a jug of water and Frankie tightens the ropes that secure the sum of their worldly possessions to the shell of the truck: bed frames . . . wash tubs . . . a crate of laying hens . . . you name it.

'Okay everyone, back in the truck,' says Ed.

'Speedy won't come, Daddy,' says Dona. The dog has wandered down the ditch and ignores Ed's whistle.

'Go fetch him, Frankie. We gotta get going.'

Frankie walks along the roadside, slides down the bank and finds Speedy pawing at a raggedy blue jacket in the few inches of water at the bottom. He kneels down for a closer look and nudges Speedy aside. Inside the jacket is a small, thin boy, cold and lifeless. A knit cap and schoolbook lie nearby. The dog looks up at Frankie and whines.

'It's okay, Speedy,' but it isn't okay at all. Speedy noses the dead boy's hand and licks his cheek, the same way he wakes the girls for school back home. Sensing something isn't quite right, Ed walks down the gravel shoulder. Frankie looks up, shakes his head and gives his father a silent communication so as not to upset his little sisters.

'Come out of the ditch, son, and leave things as they are,' he says. Frankie gathers up the dog and climbs to the road.

His youngest daughter appears above the ditch. 'Is something wrong, Daddy?'

'I want everyone back in the truck. We need to find a telephone.'

When her father uses his serious voice, she knows better than to ask why.

★ ★ ★

Angel is curled in sleep, her golden hair fanned out across the pillow, her skin fever-hot. The sheet has slipped from her shoulder and there's a four-fingered bruise on her upper arm. I ease from the bed and walk to the closet. I slide the hangers quietly along the pole and find her raincoat. The fabric is torn around the missing button. It did not fall off. It was ripped off, adding to the credibility of Tom's story. Angel is still asleep when I take the elevator to the lobby.

'Morning, Hank,' I say, pouring coffee from an urn at the desk.

'Morning, Jack. It's going to be another windy one,' he says. 'Someone dropped off Angel's lost umbrella.'

'Do you know who?'

'I was back in the office, but whoever it was dropped a line of cigarette ash as long as Jimmie Durante's nose on the counter.'

I smile. 'Would you please hold the calls to 210? Angel needs to sleep in this morning.'

'Sure nuff.'

I sit in the lounge with my coffee and cigarette and flip through the newspaper. There's a brief notice about Lulu's disappearance and a description of the car she was driving. When I finish my smoke I make the rounds of the elderly tenants to make sure they're still alive and kicking. When I check on Roland he asks if I've found his car yet. When I say no, he tells me not to come back until I have.

With the matchbook in my pocket, I drive to the station in the black Cadillac that once belonged to Axel Teague. Since dead men don't drive, the chief gave me the keys for my part in the gangster's demise. After two years of bouncing over the back roads and splashing through creek beds, it's picked up a ding or two since its glory days.

I tap on the door frame of the chief's office. 'Chief, you got a minute?'

'Come on in, Jack. Aren't you off today?' he says. 'If you're here about Lulu Barker, I got nothing new to tell you. She could be anywhere, depending on how much gas was in the tank.'

'I've got something else on my mind.'

Chief Dan Garvey is a rock-solid, good-looking man in his fifties with snow-white hair and denim blue eyes. He has six kids. All boys. He jokes that he married a Catholic girl with bad rhythm. Dan is that curious mixture of back-slapping affability and thinly disguised menace, the kind who's a good drinking buddy but someone you don't want to cross. He'd find no contradiction in going to mass on Sunday and beating a confession out of some poor slob on Monday.

'Whatcha got there?' he says.

I hand him the matchbook and smell whiskey on his breath. 'It's a license plate number. I thought you might check it out for me.'

He gives it a cursory glance and hands it back. 'Don't have to. It belongs to Leland Dietrich's Straight-Eight Auburn Speedster. Custom yellow paint, red leather upholstery. The only thing flashier is Jose Garcia's fighting cock.'

'Dietrich? Never heard of him.'

'You remember Red O'Hara though.'

'I liked him. He was a standup guy as far as bootleggers go.'

'Dietrich is married to his daughter Frances. Now that Prohibition is over she's gone legit. I hear she's worth even more than Red was in his heyday. Some people think Leland's the one did her old man in, but nobody can connect the dots.'

'What does he do?'

The chief laughs. 'As little as possible from what I hear. A little gambling; a little whoring. He used to be tight with Axel Teague.'

'That's quite a résumé.'

'You want to tell me what's going on?'

'I don't know yet.' He doesn't press me.

'You know that colonial outside of town, the one with the mile of white fencing?' he says.

'On Hilliker Road? I haven't been out that way in a while.'

'Check it out. That's where Dietrich hangs his hat.'

I follow Cork Street across the bridge, where it turns into Freedom Road. After driving through acres of orchard and patches of woodland, I swing a right onto Hilliker. A few hundred yards in, I see the long driveway that leads to the house on the hill. It's big. It's white. It has pillars like an antebellum mansion. A three-car garage is visible from the road. There's a stable and several well-maintained out-buildings and half a dozen sleek saddle horses grazing on the tender winter grass.

A black Arabian mare stands out like an elegant piece of sculpture. Even for a guy from Boston who thinks horses were born with policemen on their backs, I know a quality animal when I see one. I pull to the side of the road and kill the engine. I'm firing up my second cigarette when a car door slams at the top of the hill. The Auburn flies down the driveway and swings a right. It disappears around a curve in the road up ahead.

Hilliker Road is a horseshoe that intersects with Freedom Road on both ends. I'm about to tail him when a black DeSoto pulls out from a grove of trees a hundred yards ahead and does it for me. Seems I'm not the only one keeping tabs on the rich lady's husband. Rather than join the parade I wait a few minutes, swing a u-turn and drive back the way I came. That, however, doesn't mean I'm through with Leland Dietrich.

Wind buffets the car as I drive toward town, dead leaves blowing skyward, water hanging in the clouds. As I approach the river, the coroner's van, a converted commercial bread truck, cuts in front of me and continues south on the main highway. The first thing that crosses my mind is Lulu Barker, so I tag along.

★　★　★

When Angel opens her eyes, Jack is gone. Her head aches. She's sore and bruised, thirsty and hot. In the bathroom she washes down aspirin. Her broken shoe sits on the closet floor, the heel twisted awkwardly to the side. The shoe. The button. Jack's a detective. He notices things like that.

Despite her stiff neck and the ringing in her ears, Angel puts on grey slacks, a fluffy white sweater and silk head scarf. With the shoe in her shoulder bag, she takes the elevator to the lobby. Hank is busy loading the cigarette machine and she goes unnoticed out the door. She literally bumps into Cantor Nemschoff in the entryway. He's leaning on his silver-tipped cane, a religious book in his other hand.

'Shabbat Shalom, my dear.'

'I'm so sorry. My balance is a bit off this morning.'

'No harm done. Vere are you goink vidout a coat?'

'To Moe's. The fresh air feels good.'

'It's not fresh, it's freezink, and you don't look so good today. You need to be in bed vit chicken soup. If my wife Raisel vas alive, bless her soul, she vould fix for you.'

'I'll be fine. I just need to drop off my shoe, then I'm tucking in with my book. How are your knees today?'

'Oui! Don't ask. Come, I'll valk you on my vay to temple.'

She looks around to make sure Dietrich is nowhere in sight and figures she'll be safe walking with the cantor.

Tom is leaning against his cab, his arms crossed jauntily over his chest. He has a broad white smile and his chauffeur's cap is pushed back on his head. He shoves off the bumper as they approach. Without makeup and appearing somewhat fragile, Angel looks younger than usual, her eyes that brilliant blue that takes his breath away.

'Hop in,' he says. 'Ladies ride free today.'

'Thanks anyway, Tom, but the cantor and I are walking together. He can't ride or handle money on the Sabbath. It's against the rules.'

A racy redhead in a feathered hat and clacking Lucite bracelets steps up to the cab stand. Three cabs are at the curb, but she goes straight for Tom's. She runs her hand over his biceps as he opens the door, but he's too busy watching Angel to notice. A man with three cabs and money in the bank isn't a bad catch, he tells himself.

'Don't you think it's ironic that Temple Beth Shalom is on St. Finnbar Street?' Angel asks the cantor.

The cantor laughs and makes a helpless palms-up gesture. 'It's America. Everything mixed together like goulash.'

Five minutes later they arrive at Moe Zimmerman's Shoe Repairs.

'Remember,' says the cantor as he continues down the sidewalk, 'bed rest, chicken soup.'

9

The bell rings above the door as Angel walks into Moe Zimmerman's shop. 'Good morning, Moe.'

Moe is a short, pudgy man in his fifties, wearing a leather apron and repairing a bridle at his workbench. He walks to the counter. 'Good morning, Angel. What can I fix for you today? A broken heart? A traffic ticket?'

She laughs. 'How about a shoe?' she says, pulling it from her bag and handing it over. She's swept by a wave of dizziness and rests a hand on the counter to steady herself.

Moe examines the shoe from every angle. 'This I can fix. It will be ready in a day or two.'

'Can I pay now so Albie can pick it up for me?'

'Sure. How about two bits?'

Angel is suddenly feeling very unwell as she fishes change from her coin purse and hands it over.

'Thank you, dear,' he says and hands her a receipt.

The shoe repair shop shares a wall with the bakery. Angel had wanted to say hello to Joe and Cookie, but a pain has settled deep in her ear and she thinks better of it.

'By the way, have you heard about the new Deutschlander Social Club?' says Moe. 'They've rented a space in the auction barn.'

She turns around just short of the door, a sick feeling in the pit of her stomach, a patina of sweat breaking out on her forehead. 'I heard someone mention it. It'll be nice for you and Elsa.'

'We looked forward to making new friends, maybe sharing recipes and doing some dancing. Yesterday we see cars in the lot, so we go inside. Three men are setting up tables and a movie screen. I introduce Elsa and myself. I tell them my family came from Weimar three generations back and that my grandparents came west in a covered wagon. They speak to us in German, but the old tongue died with my parents and I don't understand but a word here and there.

Instead of the warm welcome we expect, they say membership is closed and send us away.'

'That's certainly odd.' Angel's head is swirling now, her ear throbbing painfully. She can hardly think, but she's interested in what he has to say and doesn't want to appear rude.

'They said their membership is limited by the fire code,' he continues.

'That's nonsense. There's 20,000 square feet in that barn. It could hold Napoleon's army.'

'And there aren't enough Germans in Santa Paulina to fill a corn crib.'

'What do you think is going on with them?'

'I had the feeling they didn't think we were German enough to join their club.'

'How German would you have to be?'

'I don't know. Maybe like Fritz Kuhn, spitting on American principles, then expecting the constitution to protect him.' She'd heard that name before, maybe in one of Forsythe's broadcasts.

'In that case, you'd do better to stay away from them. They don't sound like very nice people.' Angel is losing hearing in one ear, like she has a balloon expanding inside her head. 'I have to get back, Moe. I'm a little out of sorts today.'

'Well, don't let the wind blow you off course,' he says, waving her off.

The first thing she sees when she steps onto the sidewalk is Leland Dietrich's Auburn idling at the curb on the far side of Cork Street. If she walks fast, she'll be inside the Rexford before he can make a u-turn. Angel's knees threaten to give way as the sidewalk rises and falls beneath her feet. Wind steals her scarf and her hair whips around her face.

Just as the Auburn makes its move, Tom Kelly pulls to the curb. 'Angel, get in,' he calls, leaning across the seat of his cab and throwing the passenger door open. She slumps against the outer wall of the bank building and slides to the sidewalk.

Tom jumps from the cab at a sprint. He helps her up and she leans into his side.

'I feel awful,' she says. 'I don't know what's wrong with me, Tom.'

'Come on, I'll get you home.' He puts

her in the cab and climbs behind the wheel. 'You're burning up,' he says, touching her forehead with the back of his hand.

'I'm cold, very cold,' she says, with a convulsive shudder.

The Auburn makes a u-turn in traffic and slows down when it passes the driver's side of the cab. The men's eyes lock and the yellow car moves on down Cork.

'It's that same man again,' says Tom. 'What's with this guy?'

Angel whispers a few unintelligible words.

'Dr. McBane is in with Roland,' he says. 'We'll catch him before he leaves.'

Angel can't hear him. She's fallen unconscious against the passenger-side door.

When Tom carries Angel into the lobby, Hank buzzes Roland Barker's room and within seconds McBane is downstairs with his black bag. Tom follows him into the elevator with Angel limp in his arms.

'What's wrong with her, Doc?' he says, lying her on the bed.

'Get out of here so I can do my job.'

Tom gives him an imploring look. 'Please, let me stay.'

'Out. Now.'

Tom stands beneath the clock at the reception desk, not certain what to do next.

'What in god's name happened?' asks Hank.

'She was walking down the sidewalk with a roaring fever. I'm not sure she knew where she was.'

'I never saw her leave the building. I thought she was still in her room.' Hank turns back to his ledger.

'She's a sweet girl, don't you think? She's nice to everybody.'

'Yes she is,' says Hank.

'I asked Jack if I could take her to the movies, but you know how dads are about their daughters. Maybe you could put in a good word for me.'

Hank looks at Tom over his glasses and puts down his pencil. 'O-o-h boy,' he says.

'What?' says Tom.

'Forget about Angel.'

'Why would I do that? I have honorable intentions.'

'Tom, listen to me. Jack is not her father.'

Silence. The wheels turn.

'I get it. He's Dunning and she's Dahl. Jack is her stepdad.'

'No, you *don't* get it.'

Finally there's a flash of understanding in Tom's eyes. 'You've got to be kidding.'

'Just let it be.'

'But Hank, she's only a kid and he's — '

'They're together, Tom. They've been together a long time.'

'A long time! She hasn't been on this earth a long time. What is she — sixteen, seventeen? And he's, what . . . '

'Don't start with the counting, Tom. If there's one person you don't want to tangle with, it's Jack Dunning.'

* * *

Joe doesn't remember dreaming in color before. In fact, he hasn't had dreams of this nature since he was a teenager. Then again, it isn't every day a lively young creature like Miss Montoya wants to teach him how to tango. Although she isn't his type, there are times a woman like that is every man's type, whether he admits it or not.

He liberates himself from the tangled sheets and walks to the window. Although it rained vigorously during the night, the giant storm everyone's been bracing for never arrived. He didn't bother with the shutters and there's still a pile of sand and two hundred burlap bags waiting at the side of the house to be filled.

He walks down the hall toward the stairs and looks into Mildred's room. Chita was right. No woman wants to share a man with the ghost of wives past. He needs to call Stan at the second-hand store and begin packing her things up. After that he'll decide about the ashes.

Joe changes Pumpkin's litter box, puts down food and clean water and gets ready for work. Saturday is a busy day at the bakery. When he walks to his car, Happy Hooker Towing is pulling Chita's car onto the road. He waves to the driver and heads down the hill. Fifteen minutes later he's dodging the broken glass at the intersection of Cork and St. Ambrose. He parks behind the store and enters through the alley next to the stairs leading to Cookie's apartment. He puts on his white apron, sets the vat of oil bubbling and starts a fresh batch of donuts. While the coffee's brewing and the bread's rising, he takes his broom and sweeps the glass out of the street.

Back inside he lays pink napkins and paper plates at the small bistro table by the window and waits for Cookie to come down for their morning ritual of donuts and coffee. He regrets giving her a matrimonial ultimatum. It was one of the stupidest things he'd ever done.

After a twenty-minute wait, he goes up the inner stairs and knocks on her door. 'Cookie, it's me.'

No response. He tries the knob and the door drifts open. 'Cookie, it's Joe.' She's not in the parlor or the kitchen. With increasing unease he walks to the bedroom door and sees her on the floor beside the bed.

'Jesus, Mary and Joseph!' He makes the sign of the cross and rushes to her side. It isn't until he's lifted her onto the bed that he sees the plum-sized knot on her forehead. He's relieved when she moans and her eyelids flutter. At least she's alive.

'Joe,' she says. 'I've been calling for you all night.' Her voice is barely audible and she has the cloudy look of semi-consciousness. 'The horses bolted. The buckboard flipped.'

'That was a long time ago, dear. You have a big bump on your head.'

'I know. I was trapped under the wheel.'

'You lie right here. I'll get you a cup of coffee.' He's back in a flash, helping her sit up, handing her coffee with plenty of cream to cool it. He waits patiently until she's finished and sets the cup on the bed stand. 'Are you with me now?' he asks. 'It's 1936 last time I checked.'

'Don't try to confuse me with numbers.'

'Was it your heart again?'

'I was mugged, Joe. They were after my crystal ball.'

'You weren't mugged, Cookie. Your purse is on the chair and there's not a big market for crystal balls in cow country. Look at me.' He notes the swelling and bruising around her eyes, and the dark circles above her cheekbones. 'You've had one of your headaches again.'

'I should have said something yesterday, but I didn't want to be a nuisance. Joe, I had one of the strangest dreams last night.'

Joe thinks of Chita and suppresses a smile. He had a pretty strange one himself. 'Did anyone die this time — in your vision, I mean?'

'I don't know. It was interrupted by a car wreck out front.'

'Let me get you an ice bag to bring that swelling down.' Something rolls beneath his foot. He bends over and picks up a small glass bottle.

'I thought you weren't going to take this stuff anymore.'

'I only take it when I have to.'

'When I left yesterday there was an eighth of a bottle. That's at least four or five doses. Now it's empty. You're going to kill yourself with this . . . this . . . Chinese devil juice.'

'You Italians! Why do you have to turn everything into a major crisis?'

'Dr. McBane knows it's dangerous, probably deadly, the old fool.'

'If you had migraines you'd understand.'

'I know he gives you two bottles. Where's the other one?'

'None of your business.'

'All right, I'll find it myself.'

'If you do, I'll call Jack and tell him you're stealing from me. Don't think I won't.'

'Go ahead, call Jack, then Dr. McBane and Li Dock Qwan can share a jail cell. Better yet, they'll ship Qwan back to China.'

'You wouldn't dare.'

'Oh, wouldn't I?'

'I want you out of here!' She sinks back on the pillow as a sharp pain shoots behind her eyes.

Joe marches to the bathroom and gets the ice bag. He goes to the kitchen, fills it with ice and tosses it on the bed. 'Put that on your head,' he says. He returns to the bathroom and gets the second bottle of

113

elixir from the medicine cabinet. Cookie tries to get out of bed, but collapses back on the pillow.

Joe points a stern finger at her. 'You stay right where you are. I'm taking this with me,' he says, holding up the bottle. The golden liquid shimmers seductively in the light. 'I'm calling Dr. Albright to come and check you over.'

'It's Saturday.'

'I don't care if it's the Feast Day of the Immaculate Conception. I better not catch you going back to Quack McBane.'

'I hate you! You're just like Skipper. Get out of here and don't come back.'

'Let me remind you, I own this building.'

'I'm moving.'

'Then pack your crystal ball and go. What do I care?'

★   ★   ★

I follow the van past Sparkey's Roadhouse. A half-mile further we pass the schoolhouse on the same side of the highway. Another quarter mile and the coroner pulls

114

to the opposite side of the road behind a flatbed truck. Homer Platt and I exit our vehicles at the same time. I don't see Lulu's car.

'Hello, Jack. How did you get here so fast?' says Homer.

'I chase coroners like dogs chase cats. What have you got?'

'A body in the ditch is what the caller said.'

I see serpentine tire tracks along the road, but no car. 'Are we talking about an elderly woman with a red dye job and a raccoon coat?'

'Nope. A young boy from what I was told.'

Homer is a tall, bony man as pale as the corpses on his autopsy table. A year back he took over the family business from his father, who had the good sense to move to Florida.

A man in overalls with a half-grown boy at his side walks toward us. A woman sits in the cab of the truck, three little girls and a dog looking on.

'I'm Ed Thompson. This is my boy, Frank,' says the man.

'I'm Homer Platt,' says the coroner. 'We spoke on the phone. This is Officer Dunning with the Santa Paulina P.D.' We shake hands. Ed is wiry and short, but hard-muscled with knuckles like oak knots.

'Our dog is the one found the young fellow. Looks like he's been there a spell.'

'Let's have a look, Jack,' says Homer, leading the way.

We slide into the ditch. The boy, about six or seven years old, lies in a few inches of water. Not far from the body is a waterlogged schoolbook and a blue knit cap. The boy's head is scabby and shaved close to the scalp, indicating the presence of head lice. He wears a threadbare blue jacket that bears a few flakes of green on the shoulder, which reminds me again of Roland's green Chevy.

'That look like car paint to you?' I say.

'Hard to tell.'

'How long do you think he's been here?'

He feels the boy's limbs. 'Rigor's already come and gone. Since yesterday sometime. Anyone report a boy missing?'

116

'Not that I'm aware of.'

We get our cameras and shoot the scene from various angles. I take one of the zigzag tire tracks along the shoulder. We squeeze water from the boy's coat and load him into the back of the van along with the cap and schoolbook. Even wet the boy feels weightless and hollow-boned.

I walk over to Ed Thompson, get his statement, take notes. He doesn't know any more than we do. 'Unless I can be of further help, I'd like to get going,' he says. 'I have a front headlamp out, so I'd like to clear the Altamont Pass before dark.'

'Thanks for your help, and good luck to you.'

Homer heads to the mortuary and I drive to the station. The chief is out and Sergeant Boyle is on the front desk. 'Anybody report a missing schoolboy?' I ask.

'No.'

'If they do, leave a message for me at the Rexford and notify Platt. He brought a dead boy in off the highway, but we haven't I.D.ed him yet.'

'Hit and run?'

'Probably.'

'Between Sparkey's and the Kingsolvers?'

'Yes, why?'

'It's odd, that's all.'

'How so?'

'When you and Angel were vacationing back in September, another boy was found on the road. When you get more dead kids than dead dogs on the same stretch of road it makes you wonder, don't it?'

10

Joe is not himself for the rest of the day. He bumbles through his routine — dropping change, spilling a cup of coffee, burning a chocolate cake. He wanted to apologize for the mean things he said yesterday, but his opinion about the dangers of the devil juice haven't changed.

Cookie watches Joe pull into traffic at the end of the day, then goes down to the bakery for the newspaper. Dr. Albright's visit had been a waste of time. All he recommended were the things that hadn't been effective in the past. He told her to keep the ice bag on her head and charged her an extra quarter for the house call.

She sits at the bistro table and flips through the pages of the *Morning Sun*. If there's something about a murder or assault, it might explain her strange dream. There's news of foreclosures, livestock sales, a church rummage sale and a .22 slug in the gas station window. No violence, mayhem or murder. As she's folding the paper, she sees what appears to be a business card on the floor near the door. Curious, she walks over and picks it up.

CONCHITA MONTOYA

DANCE INSTRUCTOR

TOP HAT SCHOOL OF DANCE

RUMBA, SAMBA, TANGO CLASSE

SATURDAY EVENING 8:00 O'CLOCK

Cookie turns the card over and sees a penciled message on the back: 'Cho, is complimentary lesson, 11213 Railroad Spur Rd. XOX Chita'
Cho? Chita?
So, this is what Joe is up to, she thinks. Stealing her elixir, starting an argument . . . a sneaky way to justify making time with another woman. Her miserable days with Skipper come back in a sickening rush. The lies. The late nights at the office. The weekends with 'the boys.'

Shards of light slice through the neural pathways of her brain, distorting her vision to the point of partial blindness. By the time she feels her way up to the apartment, one eye is swollen shut and her head is exploding with pain.

* * *

Frances has had a bad day. And when Frances has a bad day, so does everyone around her. When Mittie, her twenty-year-old house maid, broke a Tiffany lamp, she blew her stack and banished her for the weekend. Now, she's alone with no one to talk with and coughing up more blood than usual. She's always considered herself indestructible, but just lately she has to admit to not being entirely well.

Frances lights a cigarette and pours a whiskey straight. It burns her throat going down. Like father, like daughter. If Red O'Hara smoked and drank, she smoked and drank. In her eyes, he could do no wrong, nor she in his.

Tonight she sits in the living room in

one of her darker moods, missing her father more than ever. She's never been the same since he took a bullet in the back, nor has she been able to establish with any certainty Leland's movements on the night he died.

Now that she knows that Leland isn't even Leland, her suspicions have deepened. Red wouldn't let down his guard with a stranger, but he might with his son-in-law. With their marriage unraveling, Frances is worth more dead than alive, and a bullet in the back is one tradition she doesn't intend to share with her father.

The phone rings and a vein jumps in her temple. She snatches up the receiver. 'What?' she says. A flurry of dry leaves shoots past the windowpane and a branch scraping against the house sounds like fingernails on a blackboard.

'It's Darrell Singleton, Mrs. Dietrich.'

'Yes, yes, what is it?'

'There's been a new development. I'll give it to you now and send you a written report in the morning. I'm calling from a phone booth across from the auction barn. I followed Mr. Dietrich to the German Social Club.'

'Never heard of it.'

'Tonight's their first meeting. Before the doors opened I mingled with the crowd out front.

'So?'

'Your husband met up with a young woman, but I had the feeling they weren't meeting for the first time.'

'Singleton, this is redundant. I already know he's a dog.'

'Hear me out. I didn't sense any romantic undertones this time. Of the fifty or so men in attendance, she was the only woman, so she must be someone with status. In the lot were license plates from all over the state: San Francisco . . . Fresno . . . Los Angeles . . . like this meeting was a big deal. They'd come to hear a lecture by . . . you want to take a guess?'

'Just tell me.'

'Ludwig Gerhard von Buchholz.'

It takes a moment for her to associate the name with her husband. 'You're a man of many surprises, Singleton.'

'So is your husband.'

Frances coughs a husky laugh.

'There's something else. Although Mr. Dietrich was the guest speaker, the head honcho is a man named Hansel Von Stroheim, and his license plate is out of L.A. When he arrived, his name was on everyone's lips. He looks like an Aryan god. Six foot five. Sandy blond hair. Carries himself like an Olympic athlete.'

'What, no dueling scar?'

'Left cheek. Two inches long. Either that, or he doesn't know how to use a straight razor. When he arrived the crowd was mesmerized. After he went inside security bolted the door. What I'd give to be a fly on *that* wall.'

'I don't know where all this is leading, but stay on it and see what develops.'

At midnight Frances walks to the stable, her .38 in hand. She wears jodhpurs, riding boots and a white blouse speckled with blood from all that coughing. The horses are bedded down for the night, but when Sahara Princess hears her enter, she's greeted with an excited whinny.

Princess was this year's anniversary present to Leland, but clearly he no longer deserves such a magnificent animal. She'd take everything back if she could: the Auburn . . . the fancy clothes . . . the box at the San Francisco Opera House. He shows his horse off to friends, but never gives her the amount of exercise a spirited animal requires. The black Arabian is a desert horse whose ancient pedigree is rooted in the sands of time. At a gallop her long mane and tail ripple on the wind like liquid silk.

Frances paid more for the horse than your average man makes in five years. She strokes the animal's neck and whispers into her mane. Princess nudges her right hand, but instead of a sugar cube, it holds a gun.

Frances picks up the telephone on the far wall and dials Will Bernside's home phone. He's the owner of the Consolidated Rendering Plant in Manteca — an unusual name for a town, meaning 'lard' when translated into English. Like most people at this hour, Will is sleeping.

'Do you know what time it is?' he says.

'This is Frances Dietrich, Will. I have to put down an injured horse. How soon can you pick up the carcass?'

Will is grumbly with sleep. 'Call me tomorrow at the plant. I don't take the schedule to bed with me.' He hangs up with a sharp click.

'Some people!' she says.

Princess prances and circles, impatient for her treat. Frances leans against the half-door of the stall. The mare nibbles playfully at her ear. Another whinny. Big brown eyes, bright with curiosity and intelligence. Fran's anger dissipates. She pockets the gun and gives Princess her sugar as she presses her cheek against the mare's warm neck. She fights back a tear. When she fires a bullet, it's not going to be into something as noble as a horse.

Frances brings the pickup around, puts the gun under the front seat and hooks the horse trailer to the hitch. She loads the mare for transport to another of her properties where Leland won't find her.

When her husband took it upon himself to fire their groom last year — a former jockey, who'd been ten years with the family — she'd been furious, especially when he marched away from her without explanation. Now, she knows why.

The groom was Benny Silverstein. A Jew.

Joe has a date . . . well, sort-of a date. He's filled with both trepidation and excitement as he puts on the dark suit he reserves for weddings, funerals and jury duty. It's dated, but nicely tailored to his tall, slender physique.

He fastens silver cufflinks at the wrists of his spotless white shirt, holds up a dozen ties and selects the blue one with the narrow, silver stripe to match the silver at his temples. He tilts his fedora at a rakish angle, takes a deep breath and blows it out. Gloves and a top coat and he's as ready as he's ever going to be.

On the drive to town, he reflects on Chita's parting words. 'Be honest, Cho. I know when a man is dying to play with fire. Eight o'clock. You no come, I cry like baby.' He hasn't had an invitation like this since he was on the high school basketball team. If he waits for another, he'll be too old to strike a match, let alone fan the flames.

He checks his map. Railroad Spur Road branches off to the packing house and various factories in the industrial area east of town. A quarter-mile down the road and the last streetlight vanishes in his rear-view mirror. The road is deeply rutted, his car rocking and bouncing over the pot-holes. A spray of tarred gravel strikes the undercarriage. He needn't have bothered polishing the car and scrubbing the whitewalls. He drives slowly, scanning the darkness for the dance school, but all he sees are buildings locked down for the night and the green fluorescent glow from the packing plant.

After a five-minute drive the road dead-ends at an auto supply warehouse. For a moment he sits bewildered behind the wheel. He's looking for 11213, but the numbers don't run that high.

The ever-punctual Joe is running late and there's no second chance to make a first impression. He resumes his search, growing more frustrated by the minute. At eight-forty he slams on the brakes and fishtails to a stop. With a sickening jolt he realizes there is no school of dance. There never was.

Cho has been duped!

Sweat pops in his armpits and his face flushes with embarrassment. He slaps the steering wheel with the palm of his hand. 'You stupid old fool,' he says, making a three-point turn and racing back toward home.

The front door is standing open when Joe pulls in the driveway. Two pairs of muddy footprints crisscross the porch, one small and one belonging to Bigfoot.

A trace of perfume still lingers on the air when he takes the stairs to the second floor, anxiously calling for Pumpkin. He rushes to his bedroom, then the guest room and finally Mildred's room, where his traumatized cat crawls out from under the bed with his fur standing on end and his eyes as big as moons.

He sweeps the cat into his arms and holds him so close he can feel Pumpkin's rapid heartbeat. After a few minutes

Pumpkin begins to purr and Joe sets him on the bed. Mildred's clothes are scattered across the floor. Her furs and expensive shoes are gone, along with the silver brush and mirror set, M being for Montoya and all. In its place is a note: *Sorry Cho. You nice man. In future no be so trusting. Scatter ashes. No good for finding new wife.*

Quite the felonious little philosopher!

Pumpkin follows Joe to his bedroom. His personal possessions are intact. Apparently Bigfoot couldn't get into his size-nine shoes. He recalls the items in Chita's car: the guitar, the candlesticks, the gun case. Now, he wonders whose house she burglarized before sliding off the road.

Joe decides against reporting the burglary. He should, but he won't. It would be in the newspaper and he doesn't want Cookie to know what an old fool he's been. Even if she never speaks to him again, it's important she thinks well of him.

Joe locks his doors for the first time in forty years, although it's a little late to do him any good. He hangs his suit in the closet until the next wedding or funeral and gets into his striped pyjamas. Between his flap with Cookie, burning the cake and being scammed by a flirtatious young tart, it's been a very trying day.

He crawls beneath the covers and Pumpkin hops on his chest. There's a small snap of electricity as they touch noses. When the purring and treading begin, Joe gives him a firm hug and tucks him into the crook of his arm. For a long time he lies staring at the ceiling. Tomorrow after mass, he'll drive to the coast of Big Sur where he and Mildred spent their honeymoon. From the cliff tops, he'll release her ashes into the wind above the sea.

★ ★ ★

Hank motions me over as soon as I walk into the lobby. It's dark outside and the wind is moaning between the buildings. He tells me Angel was seen by Dr. McBane that afternoon and he sedated

131

her so she could rest.

'Did he say what's wrong?'

'A winter bug of some kind. She's to rest, drink water and take aspirin. He'll check on her later in the week. Anything new on Lulu?' Hank asks.

I shake my head. 'It's not looking good.'

'That's a damn shame.' He looks at me like he has something else to say, but the moment passes and I walk to the elevator.

11

The meeting of the Deutschlander Social Club breaks up a couple hours after midnight, men pouring out the door, laughing and back-slapping, everyone in high spirits as they head to their cars. During the meeting Singleton had walked through the empty parking lot, jotting down license numbers in his notebook.

After the others are gone, Dietrich and the mystery woman linger in the lot as Singleton watches from his vantage point near the phone booth. The couple talks for the length of time it takes to smoke two cigarettes, relaxed in one another's company, no intimate touching or sexual overtures. His feet are numb with cold and he yearns for the comforts of his motel room — a long shower, a warm bed, a nightcap. He doubts that anything of further significance will happen tonight.

Finally, the two comrades flick their cigarette butts into the darkness. They salute and click their heels with a hearty 'Heil Hitler' and leave in separate cars. If they only knew how ridiculous they looked.

Singleton is about to call off surveillance when Dietrich pulls onto Cork Street and drives in the opposite direction of Hilliker Road. Another foray into Chinatown? he wonders. He closes the notebook containing the license numbers he collected while the meeting was in session. The nightcap and warm bed will have to wait. He keys his car. It coughs a couple times before the engine kicks over. He checks the gas gauge. It hovers near 'E' but the stations are closed. He's curious and decides to risk it. Besides, his vigilance might earn him a nice fat bonus from the rich Mrs. Dietrich.

The P.I. lets his subject get a head start before he pulls into the empty street. He prefers tailing subjects in moderate traffic, but sometimes you have to take it as it comes. The job that began as surveillance of an adulterous spouse has turned into something a little out of his line. Nevertheless, he'd like to wrap things up in another day or two and get back home to his wife and kids.

After a mile or so Dietrich pulls off Cork onto St. Finnbar Street. What the hell is on St. Finnbar Street that could possibly be of interest to Leland Dietrich? He passes the Catholic church and adjacent parochial school with its empty playground and baseball diamond. With the exception of a dim light above the rectory door, the street is dark, leaves piling up in the gutters, wind rattling the chains on the swings.

Dietrich pulls to the curb in front of the Jewish synagogue and a bad feeling creeps into Singleton's bones. He passes him at a crawl, makes a u-turn and parks up the street. He kills the lights and turns off the engine. Dietrich exits his car and disappears behind the building. The unpainted structure is old and weathered, the architecture like something out of an Eastern European shtetl.

He waits for Dietrich to reappear, then waits some more, his back muscles aching, one foot gone slightly numb. What the hell is Dietrich doing back there? He catches movement in the rear-view mirror, someone walking his dog or having a last smoke before turning in. It's only when the shadowy figure gets closer that he realizes Dietrich has circled behind the buildings and come up behind him.

Singleton keys the ignition. Nothing. He tries again. His car lets out a mechanical groan but refuses to kick over. He tries again and again, rapidly pumping the gas pedal. What little gas is left in the tank floods the engine and the car fills with fumes. Another glance in the rear view mirror and Dietrich is coming toward him at a trot.

Singleton grabs his keys and notebook, jumps from the car and hits the ground. He goes full out for a block, his lungs aching from the cold night air. In the deep shadow of a giant oak tree, he drops the notebook and keys into a curbside mailbox, barely breaking his stride. He bolts down the sidewalk without looking back. If he had, he'd see that Dietrich was holding a gun.

* * *

Angel is asleep when I crawl into bed. I smooth the damp hair from her forehead and feel her soft breath on my shoulder. Her nightgown is inside-out, the tag visible at the neckline. She shivers and fever-talks in her sleep and I wonder how much of her suffering is due to fever and how much to her encounter with Leland Dietrich.

I drift off. I'm not sure how long I'd been sleeping when I feel a hand on my shoulder. I open my eyes and see Angel standing beside the bed.

'What is it?' I say, sitting up. 'Are you all right?'

'Jack, something's going on.' She takes my hand and pulls me to the window. 'Look,' she says. 'Over there, above the rooftops.' The sky to the east blooms with a flickering orange glow. A fire truck, its sirens screaming, flies past the hotel. I hear footsteps in the hall, the murmur of voices, the elevator rattling up and down. 'Let's find out what's going on,' she says. 'Please, help me with my robe.'

The lobby is abuzz with people in nightclothes. Jake, Albie and Cantor Nemschoff stand in a shivering crowd gathered on the sidewalk out front. Angel is weak and leans more heavily on my arm. 'I think I'd better sit,' she says.

'You should be in bed. Let me take you back up.'

'Not yet, Jack. Go see what's happening first.'

I get her settled in the lounge and join the people at the curb. Wind whips the distant flames hundreds of feet into the air, sirens pulsing in the distance.

'That's one hell of a fire,' says Jake.

'That was going to be my school,' says Albie, as Bo snores softly in his arms. 'St. Finney's is burning down.'

Cantor Nemschoff, wrapped in his blue-and-white prayer shawl, is pale and shaken, his hand trembling on his cane. 'No,' he says, 'that's the synagogue. It's starting all over again, just like back in Germany.'

12

Saguaro Correctional

In the chilly dawn, Hedy Greiss shows Head Administrator Horace Churchwell the key ring Penelope Hanover left in the records room. Together they walk down the path to Bungalow 5. The door is locked and scattered coins lie among shattered pieces of glass from the petty cash jar. Very incriminating. Just the way Hedy planned it.

'She must have panicked when she realized she didn't have her key,' says Horace.

'And her car is gone from the parking area,' adds Hedy.

'But look, her car key is on the ring,' he says.

'She keeps a spare in the glove compartment because she's always misplacing things. She's very sweet, but you know how scatterbrained she can be.'

'Well, let's hope she returns. She may have a reasonable explanation for her behavior.'

Hedy smiles. There is one, but Horace Churchwell is never going to hear it. 'She's an excellent teacher. I'd hate to lose her before the semester is over. If you'd woken me during the night, Miss Greiss, she might have had an opportunity to explain herself.'

'I realize that now. Penny thought she could handle the isolation of the desert, but with no movie theater, no place to shop and no marital prospects she'd become disillusioned.'

'She told you that?'

'Oh yes, on more than one occasion. She talked often of returning to the city.'

'Well, let's give it a day or two and see what happens. I'll have Jesus clean up the glass. By the way, with all the midnight oil you're burning, I hope you're ready for the state audit.'

'You needn't worry, Mr. Churchwell. I'm on top of it.'

13

Angel and I listen to the morning news. Her fever has dropped to 100 degrees, her bad ear resting on a heating pad. 'Feeling any better?' I ask.

'Better than yesterday. So, Cantor Nemschoff was right. It was the synagogue that burned. Do you think he was right about things starting over?'

'You mean Nazis? I know they're spreading their poison in a lot of places, but why target a speck on the map like Santa Paulina?'

'Think, Jack. It's our central location that attracts them. We're a hub with spokes reaching out to San Francisco, Los Angeles, Stockton and Sacramento, seats of money and influence. We're easily reached by train, Greyhound or a day's drive.'

'That makes sense, but the first thing the fire inspector is going to look at is the frayed wiring in that old fire trap, not arson.'

The phone rings and I pick up. By the time I hang up, Angel knows we won't be spending Sunday in bed.

'I know that look, Jack.'

'You're right. Homer wants me down at the mortuary.'

'Oh no, not Lulu.'

'It's about the boy we found on the road.'

'Poor little fellow,' Angel says.

'I might be late, so have Albie pick something up for you at the Memory Lights. Are you going to be okay?'

'Sure. Don't worry about me.' She goes silent and just looks at me, all blue-eyed and thoughtful. I think she's about to tell me about Leland Dietrich, but I'm wrong.

'I've been thinking about the dining room off the lobby,' she says.

'The dining room? What about it?'

'When Hank bought the place, the dining room had been closed off for years, but there are still tables and chairs and a full kitchen in the back. It would be nice if it were up and going again, no more running back and forth to the café in bad weather.'

'It would be nice.'

'I'm going to talk to Hank about it.'

'I like the idea, but it would take a lot of work. He'd need a license, a cook, a dish-washer . . . '

'You're not following me, Jack. I'd manage the dining room myself. One meal a day at dinnertime. I could set it up buffet-style, make it really nice with flowers on the tables — chili and hotdogs one night, chicken or meatloaf the next. A lot of our older residents don't eat right because it's either hard for them to get out or the cost is too high. I think some of them go hungry more often than we know.'

'You manage the dining room?'

'Don't look so surprised. I've given it a lot of thought.' She tries to rise on an elbow, then, dizzy and weak, sinks back on the bed.

'Are you sure this isn't the fever talking?'

'I'm capable of clear thinking, Jack. I can't continue living off of you and being your . . . whatever it is I am . . . without doing something constructive with my life. Otherwise, I'm just taking up space on the planet. You've got your job. Hank has his hotel. Even Albie has his newspapers. I'm like everybody else. I need to do something useful in this world.'

★ ★ ★

I have an unsettled feeling in the pit of my stomach as I drive toward the mortuary. Angel's message had as much to do with our relationship as with flowers and meatloaf. I had no idea she felt the way she did.

Whatever it is I am.

It was painful to hear those words and it's my fault she had to say them. I've been given a second chance for happiness and I'm afraid to own it, not because I don't love Angel, but because I screwed up so badly in my first marriage. I'd turned Sandra from a trusting young woman into a shrike who hated me almost as much as I hated myself. I didn't want to risk doing the same thing to Angel.

Now, I'm in control of my drinking, or at least I think I am, but it's a daily struggle to keep it from getting out of hand. In fact, I could go for a shot right now. When Angel said she needed *something* of her own, I think she really meant *someone* of her own, someone ready to get off the fence and make the kind of commitment that requires a justice of the peace and a ring.

Whatever it is I am. Those words haunt me.

Today, if I get killed on the job, Angel has no legal standing. In the eyes of the law, we're simply 'shacked up'. Everyone at the Rexford loves her, but it's a wide world and Angel has to live in it, hopefully with a modicum of dignity.

Then there's Tom, a good young man who doesn't lug around the baggage I do. If I were noble, I'd step aside, but I'm not that selfless. On the other hand, if I don't make a decision, someone will make it for me and I probably won't like it.

★　★　★

'Murder? You mean hit and run, don't you? Negligent homicide?'

'No, the old-fashioned, premeditated kind,' says Homer.

I shiver and rub my arms. It's freezing in the basement morgue of the old Victorian house on Cedar Street. The air smells sharply of formaldehyde, which conjures up a lot of unpleasant images, starting with dissecting frogs in high school biology.

'What about the paint on the jacket?' I say, still thinking about Roland's green sedan.

'Poster paint. The kind kids use in school.'

'Hmm.' There are two autopsy tables in the room. The boy is under a sheet nearest the entrance. An elderly man is on the one against the back wall.

'Who's his neighbor?' I ask.

'Wexler Culken. A couple nights ago Wex was coming home from his eightieth birthday party when he was broadsided by a drunk. Happened over on Cork and St. Ambrose. The man who hit him was treated for a broken thumb. I'd rather have the other guy on the table, but you

146

take 'em as they come.' Homer walks over and covers the dead man's face with a sheet. 'Wex gets his send-off tomorrow. You look a little pale, Jack. You sure you're up to this?'

'I'd rather be home reading the funny papers if that's what you mean.'

Homer laughs and snaps on his rubber gloves. 'Okay, let's get it done. I'll show you what I found.'

We step up to the table and he pulls back the sheet. The boy has a freckled face and elfin ears. He would have been a cute kid before he ended up on a slab. His stomach is sunken and I can count his ribs. I see no blood. No bullet holes. No stab wounds.

'He's about seven years old and pitifully undernourished,' says Homer.

'I see a few bruises like kids get on the playground and an abrasion on the bridge of his nose, but it doesn't strike me as significant,' I observe. 'I don't see an obvious cause of death. If he wasn't hit by a car, my second guess would be hypothermia due to lack of body fat and exposure to the elements. What am I missing?'

'I found something I should have looked for when the other boy came to me back in September,' Homer answers. 'I put the first case down as blunt force trauma due to hit and run, because internal injuries aren't always apparent on external examination and an autopsy was against his parents' beliefs. Now, I'm having second thoughts.' He lifts the boy's eyelids with gloved fingers, first one then the other. His once-blue eyes are bulged and frosted over in death, the whites webbed with burst capillaries, something I'd seen dozens of times as a homicide detective in Boston.

'Okay, I'm on board,' I say. 'Petechial hemorrhaging.'

'Yes, check this out,' Homer says. He raises the boy's upper lip. Like so many poor children, his teeth are decayed at the gum line. There are swollen lacerations where the teeth bit the underside of both upper and lower lips.

'He was suffocated.'

'Yes,' says Homer. 'Something was held with force over his face — a hand, a pillow, something of that nature. He was

148

too fragile to put up much of a fight.'

'Now the abrasion on his nose makes sense. Do you know his identity yet?'

'Not a clue. I looked for a name in his book but it was too waterlogged. Whoever he is, he probably goes to the one-room schoolhouse, but there won't be anyone there until tomorrow.'

'If he was murdered elsewhere and dumped, it would likely be from a car,' I say. 'That suggests adult involvement either in the crime, after the fact, or both.'

'I agree. Schoolyard bullies would have taken his nickel. Could have been his parents. Wouldn't be the first time we came across a throwaway kid.'

A full minute passes while I mull things over and Homer makes a few notes in the chart. 'His parents don't know he's missing,' I say.

'How do you figure?'

'He died on Friday. I don't think he was going home after school, maybe to a friend's or relative's. That's why we haven't heard anything.'

'Who'd want to kill a kid? Where's the motive?'

'Was he molested?'

'There's no indication of that.'

'What's the other boy's name, the one back in September?'

'Danny Battle. Eight years old. Third grade. Found on the same stretch of road under similar circumstances.'

'Homer, I'd like to review everything you have on both boys, including postmortem photos.'

'Okay, but I'll need the records back in a day or two.' The phone rings and Platt answers. He listens, shakes his head and hangs up.

'Looks like they've found your Chevy, Jack. A rancher discovered it a hundred feet down a ravine about seven miles outside town. A tow truck is on the way to pull it out.'

'And Mrs. Barker?'

'I'm sorry, Jack. Her body's in the car. You want to follow me out?'

I give it a moment's consideration. 'I think I'd like to focus on the boy right now. I'm going to have a look around the schoolhouse. I'll call you later.'

'Okay. Let me get those records.'

14

The empty schoolhouse, with its peeling paint, sits in the center of a soggy, weed-choked lot. To the right of the building is a teeter-totter, a tire swing and a sandbox filled with water and dead leaves. Beyond the playground, an apple orchard rolls toward the horizon. I drive over a short bridge on the left and park on Schoolhouse Road, an unpaved lane that runs back to a cluster of wood-frame houses at the dead end. Behind a row of collapsing sunflowers at the back of the lot stands an outhouse, its door sagging on rusty hinges.

I walk up the steps to the locked door, unfold a blade from my pocket knife and slide it between the door and the frame. The metal tongue moves, the door squeaks open and I step inside. The room would be cozy on school days, the potbellied stove snapping with kindling and fluttering with flames. Today it's colder than a meat locker. Behind the teacher's desk is a blackboard where she's written her name in the upper left-hand corner: Miss Hanover. Below is a list of spelling words, the word 'misspell' mis-spelled with a single s . . . a common enough mistake, but not one made by a parochial school graduate like myself, who can spell excommunication, purgatory and fornication with scholastic ease.

There's a draft as the door opens and closes behind me, admitting a girl with long brown braids, wide hazel eyes and a Band-Aid on one knee. 'Who are you?' she says.

'Jack Dunning. And you?'

'Rebecca Smallwood. I get in the same way you do.'

'Whatever works, right?' Her bare arms are covered with goose bumps. 'You look cold.'

'I know. My parents make me go outside when they fight. I didn't have time to grab my coat.'

'Sounds like they're the ones who need the cooling off.' That gets a smile. 'You go to school here?'

'Yes. I'm in sixth. I'm the smartest kid in school, even smarter than the eighth-graders. My grandfather donated the land the school sits on.'

'Consider me duly impressed.'

'Just don't eat the candy bar in Miss Hanover's desk or she'll think it was me.'

'Why is that?'

'Why do you think?'

'I see. You know where I can find her?'

'Not until tomorrow. She'll be here around seven thirty. You're that cop from Boston. I've seen you with Jim Tunney. What are you doing here?'

'Do you know where your teacher lives?'

'In town somewhere. Miss Brown boarded with my family. She was our teacher since I was in first grade, but she retired. Most teachers are too poor to rent a place of their own.'

'Who's your favorite, Miss Brown or Miss Hanover?'

'Miss Brown was nice. She got too old to remember our names, but she'd never misspell 'misspell'.'

'You noticed that too. Did you point it out?'

'To Miss Hanover? Are you kidding? I'm stuck with her until June.'

'Do you know her address in town?'

'No. My parents say I'm not allowed to ask grown-ups personal questions. If I could I'd ask her why she's twenty-three and doesn't have a husband yet. My mom says if you're not married by twenty-five, you'll be an old maid for life.'

'What's Miss Hanover's first name? I'll look her up in the book.'

'It's Penelope, like the weaver in the Odyssey, but I already looked and she's not listed.'

'You *are* smart. Did you learn that in school?'

'In the library.'

Through the window I see a woman coming down Schoolhouse Road, her eyes swollen, her red hair in a tangle.

'You know a lady with dark brown hair and yellow rain boots?'

'That's my mom. I'd better go so I don't get in trouble.'

'Which house is yours?'

'The grey one at the end of the road with the goat shed in back.'

I fish a card from my wallet and hand it to her. 'Here, keep this. Call me if you get in trouble and I'll put in the fix.'

She puts it in her pocket. 'Thanks, I will.' I smile to myself as she heads out the door.

Now that I'm alone, I go straight for the teacher's top desk drawer, hoping to find a class photo or a list of students' names and addresses. It's locked. I'd crack it open, except I've already blown my cover. The other drawers contain office supplies and test papers. I drive back to the location where the boy's body was found. I look into the ditch from the berm and out across the orchard behind it. I don't know what I'm looking for and I don't find it.

* * *

I'm having a hamburger and fries at Sparkey's Roadhouse when the phone rings. Sparkey Bohannon is a big man, an okay guy, who serves a simple menu of satisfying food and runs hookers out of trailers behind the restaurant. The chief says to turn a blind eye as long as the ladies are of age and don't get rowdy.

'It's Jim,' says Sparkey, handing me the phone.

'The dead boy's parents just left Platt's and they're on their way to the station. Their son is Georgie Allen. They know where and when he was found, but none of the details. How fast can you get here?'

I finish my beer in one breath, grab my keys and head out the door.

* * *

Hayden and Priscilla Allen are first cousins with identical powder-blue eyes and hair that resembles dandelion fluff. They're young and undernourished, their clothes threadbare from seasons of wear and endless laundering. I express my condolences, ask questions and answer questions, take notes and let them talk. Jim sits quietly off to the side, taking notes.

They were married at fourteen in the isolated mountain community in West Virginia where they were born. Georgie, not George, age seven, was born a year later. They came to California to get Hayden out of the coal mines. They wanted a better life and didn't find it. They live in an army tent behind Amos Duncan's peach orchard where they picked at harvest time. Their car is broken down and they've been unable to find steady work. Today they're driving Dunk's pickup.

'When was the last time you saw Georgie?' I ask.

'Friday morning when he left for school,' says Hayden. 'He should be in second grade, but Miss Hanover put him back a year. After school he was going to his friend Kenny Geiger's house, but when he didn't come home this morning, we went looking for him. The Geigers say he never arrived.'

'But they knew he was coming.'

'Yes.'

'What did they think when he didn't show?'

'They thought he was with us,' says Priscilla.

'When did Kenny last see Georgie?'

'They were running down the highway

157

toward Kenny's. Kenny turned around and Georgie was gone, just vanished, he said.'

Hayden, who'd been staring at his hands, looks up and gives me a riveting stare. 'All this talk is a waste of time. Shouldn't you be out looking for the person what run down my son?'

'We're already working on the case, sir. We're waiting for the official cause of death, and that can only come from the coroner's office.'

'Official cause of death! It seems pretty damn obvious, don't it? He was found in a ditch by the road. It ain't like he fell from an airplane.'

'Please try to be patient and let us do our job the right way.'

Hayden shoots a glance at his wife, who sits with her hands folded in her lap. He turns back to me. 'I know how these things work. You're protecting some local big shot who's probably never had a sober day in his life. You think we're just a bunch of hillbillies you can push around?'

'No, I don't think that.'

Priscilla puts a hand over her mouth,

one tear rolling down her cheek. With her other hand she touches Hayden's elbow in a cautionary gesture. He takes a deep breath. His face is pale, his hands trembling.

'I'm sorry,' he says. 'I was out of line.' He shakes his head. 'I don't know how we're going to tell his grandparents back home.' He chokes out a sob. 'They warned us about moving away from our kin. Now we got nothing, not even our son. I don't even know how we're going to get him buried.'

'I can't say I know the depth of your grief, Mr. Allen, but, we're here to help you. We're on the same team,' I say. 'No one wants to resolve this case more than we do. I know this isn't easy, but I need to ask you a difficult question. Do you or your son have any enemies?'

15

Jim and I take separate cars to the Geigers'. We introduce ourselves and settle on the flowered sofa in the front room. Kenny's mother, Kay, brings us coffee and cookies.

'My special coconut macaroons,' she says.

'Thank you, Mrs. Geiger. That's very thoughtful,' says Jim.

'They'll stick in your teeth,' says Harry, who sits in a broken-down easy chair with cigar ashes, magazines and newspapers scattered at his feet. It's the only untidy place in the otherwise orderly room.

'It didn't keep *you* from wolfing down the first dozen,' Kay teases. She sits across from me in a rocking chair. 'I imagine this is about Georgie. Mr. and Mrs. Allen were here earlier. Have you found the boy yet?'

'The boy is dead, Mrs. Geiger. He was found in a ditch alongside the highway,' I say.

'Oh my god!' she says. 'Is this about

that drunk driver everyone is talking about?'

'That's one of the possibilities we're looking into.'

'What other possibilities could there be?' says Harry.

'What's your line of work, Mr. Geiger?' asks Jim.

Geiger's chest puffs up. 'I'm with Cooley Sand and Gravel. I make sure the trucks get out on schedule and nobody cheats the time clock.'

'Tote that barge. Lift that bale.'

'That's right,' says Harry cheerfully. 'It's a thankless job, but someone's got to do it.'

'Harry married into the family business,' says Kay. 'I'm Wild Bill Cooley's daughter.'

'It's a lucky man has a job in these hard times,' says Jim, playing the diplomat. But we know what the men at Cooley's must think of him, riding into management on his father-in-law's coat-tails, lording it over more capable and experienced men.

'When exactly did Georgie die?' asks Kay.

'The coroner thinks it was mid- to late afternoon on Friday,' I say.

'Well, I guess that's no surprise, given he never made it here. It's tragic, just tragic.'

'If Kenny's here, we'd like to have a word with him.'

'He's dozing in his room. He's come down with an ear ailment, some kind.'

'You don't think *he* done it, do you?' laughs Harry.

'Shut up, Harry!' says Kay. 'You never know when to keep your big mouth shut.' She looks at me with a worry line between her eyebrows. 'You won't upset him, will you?'

'I'll tread lightly, I promise.'

She leaves the room and returns with a feverish little boy in flannel pyjamas printed with cowboys and bucking broncos. Kay sits back in her chair and makes room for Kenny, who rests his head against her side. 'Kenny, this is Officer Jack and that's Officer Jim.'

'Hello,' he says. 'Did you find Georgie?'

'We're making progress in the investigation,' I tell him. 'Can you help us by answering a few questions?'

'Sure.'

'Tell me the very last time you laid eyes on Georgie and what you two were doing at the time.'

'It was when school let out for the weekend. We were running along the road.'

'Toward your house?'

'Yes. A car came down the highway. A real junker. The tail pipe was dragging on the ground. Georgie and I ran into the orchard near the school. We were laughing our heads off. We hid in the trees in case it jumped the ditch. When the car was gone, I turned around and Georgie was gone too. I thought he was goofing around.'

'And you didn't see him after that, in the orchard or walking along the road?'

'No, I looked. His mom even gave him a nickel so we could go to the movies. It's all we talked about all week.'

'Let's say it like it is,' says Harry, lighting a cigar. 'The kid comes here for a warm meal and a clean bed. You know what it's like with their kind.'

163

'A warm meal and a clean bed are nice things to have, Harry,' says Kay.

Jim and I exchange a glance and ignore him. 'And that's the last time you saw or heard from him?' I ask.

'The very last,' says Kenny.

'Was anybody else in the orchard that day?'

'A few of the other kids.'

'How about adults?'

'No.'

'Tell me, Kenny, does anyone at school pick on your friend? Was he afraid of anyone? Has he ever been ganged up on, or roughed up?'

'Mostly everyone stays away from him. He talks funny cuz of where he's from, like you, but different. He has to wear a cap in school and sit at the back of the room cuz of his cooties.'

'It's, *because*, Kenny, not cuz,' says Kay.

'You mean due to his head lice?' I ask.

'Yes, becuz of that. Some people think he's dumb, but he's just shy and don't talk much. He's smarter when you get to know him.'

164

'I bet he is. Are you in the same grade?'

'Just the same age. I'm in second. Georgie's repeating first.'

'What do you think happened to Georgie?'

'I don't know. When I see him, I'll ask him and let you know.'

I look at Kay. 'I understand the teacher lives in town. Do you know where?'

'No. I thought she was boarding with the Smallwoods, like Miss Brown did.'

'Thank you for talking with us,' I say. 'Here's my card. Call us if you think of anything else. I hope you're feeling better soon, Kenny. Is there anything else you'd like to add before we go?'

'Yes. Can I hold your badge?'

★ ★ ★

Jim and I walk to our cars. 'They don't seem to be hiding anything,' says Jim.

'Something happened in that orchard,' I say.

'Could be. I promised Curley I'd stop by his house today.'

'I got him some bubblegum and auto

magazines. Hang on and I'll get them out of the car.'

After Jim leaves I spend the next half hour walking the orchard where Georgie was last seen. It's on the opposite side of the road from where his body was found. More puzzling is the fact his body lay south of the school. Whoever dumped him made it look like he was struck walking home, when in fact he was headed in the opposite direction toward the Geigers'.

I stand in the cold, hunched into the collar of my jacket in the middle of a fruitless orchard. Between the rows of bare apple trees the schoolhouse is visible from a great distance to the south. To the north the rows converge at the vanishing point. I search the ground for clues and find none. I wait for an epiphany that doesn't come. I believe the blood of the innocent cries from the ground like it says in the Bible. It's my job to listen for it.

16

Mittie knocks lightly and enters Frances's bedroom, carrying a breakfast tray and the Sunday paper. She sets it on the bed stand and raises the window shade, letting in a painful stiletto of light.

Frances moans and turns away from the window. 'Oh, must you? It's the middle of the night.'

'It's eleven a.m., Mrs. D. Time to rise and shine.' Mittie is cute and vivacious and far too cheerful in the morning.

'I thought I fired you until tomorrow.'

'Tomorrow is my regular day off and I plan to take it. My fiancé just passed the bar and we're going to celebrate. Besides, you've had plenty of time to get over your snit about the lamp.'

Frances reaches for her cigarettes. 'I suppose I have. I never should have hired you. Pretty girls either get married or end up in bed with my husband.'

'The latter never occurred to me,

ma'am.' Mittie is used to this kind of banter. In fact, she likes Frances. 'There was a big fire last night. If you lived in town you would have heard all the sirens.'

'Really? Do you know what burned?'

'The radio says Temple Beth Shalom. Reporters from the *Star* were there, so it should be in the paper. It was a complete loss from what I hear. They were lucky it didn't spread to St. Finnbar's with all the wind we had last night.' Mittie sets the breakfast tray in front of her. 'His royal highness made it home last night. His car was in the garage when I got here this morning.' Singleton always lets her know when Leland is on his way to the house. Fran wonders if she slept through his call.

'Well let's make the most of it.'

Mittie withdraws an envelope from her apron pocket and hands it to Frances. 'No one picked up the mail yesterday. This was still in the box.'

'Thank you, Mittie.'

'Do you want me to bring Mr. D. a tray?'

'I wouldn't bother unless he asks. Go

dust something while I finish waking up.'

After Mittie leaves, Frances sips her morning coffee, has a second cigarette and reads about the fire. When she's through she rips open the bank statement. She's stunned to see a dramatic decline in their joint checking balance. One large check had been written and the rest of the money drawn out in cash at the teller's window. Frances is livid and breaks into a painful coughing spell. This is one more thing she needs to discuss with Darrell Singleton.

*   *   *

Leland never felt fear like he had last night, the kind that rocks your core and seeps into the marrow of your bones like a malignancy. Sure, he'd been rattled by Fu Gang's bullets, but he'd had so much adrenaline coursing through his blood that he didn't have time to think until the danger had passed.

But last night, everything that could go wrong, did. What he'd intended as a simple arson got complicated. He'd first

169

noticed the black DeSoto a few days before. It's a small town. No big deal. The second time seemed coincidental, but when the same vehicle followed him onto St. Finnbar Street, he felt spider legs on the back of his neck.

He'd most likely been hired by Frances to document 'unhusbandly' behavior, but if this was about Red, he could as easily have been the target of a hit. The chase had been brief but exhausting, and Leland would have lost if his bullet hadn't been faster than the man could run.

A pat-down had produced a P.I. license. The man was Darrell Singleton, Pinkerton Investigator out of San Francisco, not a hit man after all. Oh well, so there's one less snoop in the world. He'd wanted to put the body in the Dodge and leave it near the town dump beside a couple of junked cars, but he couldn't find the key to Singleton's car. After checking the man's pockets and turning the interior of the vehicle upside down, he figured it had been lost in the chase. And what about Singleton's notes? P.I.s were known to document every sneeze and burp and Dietrich couldn't as much as find a scribble on the back of a grocery receipt.

With his options limited, he dragged the body to the back porch of the synagogue. He was shaking so badly he splashed gasoline on his clothes and almost set himself on fire when he dropped the match. If he's lucky, the body will go undetected for days. If he's luckier, it will be unidentifiable when it's found among the ashes.

His bad luck seemed to start with that little hooker from Cork Street, the one with the long memory and smoldering grudge. Maybe she'd made good her threat and stirred things up with Frances. Worse yet, when he imagines her giving graphic testimony in front of a grand jury in all her wounded, blue-eyed innocence, he actually trembles with fear.

⋆　⋆　⋆

After a sleepless night, Leland goes down the stairs to the kitchen where Mittie is polishing silver. 'Good morning, Mr. D.'

she says. 'Would you like me to fix you something?'

'Just coffee. I'll get it myself.' He pours a cup from the pot on the burner and sits at the end of the kitchen nook. His hair is uncombed and there's a day's growth of bristle on his jaws. 'Have you collected the mail this morning?' he asks.

'Yes sir.'

'Anything from the bank?'

'I wouldn't know, sir.'

'When the statement arrives, I want you to bring it directly to me.'

'Yes, Mr. D.'

When he turns his back she sticks out her tongue at his retreating form.

17

Jim and I pull up to the school at 7:30 the next morning. The teacher stands by the door, preparing to call the children in from the playground. An elegant grey Studebaker Dictator is parked off to the side.

The teacher doesn't match the car. She's not *un*attractive, just buckboard-plain . . . long skirt . . . brooch at her high-collared, long-sleeved blouse.

'Miss Hanover?' I say as we approach.

'Yes. Good morning,' she says, her smile slightly tentative.

'I'm Officer Jack Dunning and this is my partner, Jim Tunney.'

'Pleased to meet you both, I'm sure. If the Wheelers' cow has wandered off again, she hasn't come this way.'

'We're here on a more serious matter. We need to talk in private.'

'Now?' She glances behind her at the clock on the classroom wall. 'Class commences in five minutes.'

'Let them play a while,' says Jim.

'Please come out of the cold, gentlemen.' We step over the threshold. The interior is slightly smoky, the woodstove grinding out heat. 'What can I do for you? We have tests scheduled so I'm a little pressed for time.'

'We just have a question or two,' I say.

'Is this about the reckless driver? He almost ended up in the ditch out front.'

'We're here in regard to a student.'

'Oh dear, I hope none of my children are in trouble.'

'One of your students is dead, Miss Hanover,' I say. 'His body was found in the ditch down the highway on Saturday. He'd been lying there since late Friday.'

There's a stunned silence broken by an impassioned, 'Who?'

'Georgie Allen.'

'Oh my God! Poor child. A hit and run?'

'The cause is under investigation.'

'What else could it possibly be?'

'When did you see him last?'

'He was in attendance on Friday.'

'Did he have a problem with anyone?

Ever see him bullied or ganged up on?'

'Of course not. I'd never tolerate such a thing.'

'Did he have any enemies?'

'Children do not have enemies. He was a quiet little boy who kept to himself.'

'When did you last lay eyes on him?'

'What do you mean?'

'Did you actually see him go through the door after school? Did you see which way he went?'

'No. I had my back turned. I was erasing the math problems from the blackboard as the children left. Then I got in my car and drove home.'

'And where would that be?' I ask.

'Home, you mean? Stella Bloch's boarding house, 287 Cleveland Street.'

'So you don't board with a student like Miss Brown did?'

'I like my privacy. When you live with a family their problems become your problems.' She glances at the clock. There's something a little off about Miss Hanover, but I can't put my finger on it.

'Cleveland is a pretty run-down area.'

'I was new in town and only had a few

days to get settled before school started. I took the first place I looked at.'

'Georgie's parents tell us you set him back a grade,' says Jim.

'Yes, that's correct. If a student doesn't grasp the essentials we can't keep kicking the can down the road. Certainly you see the logic in that.'

'And the school board was in compliance?' asks Jim.

'The school board.' She rolls her eyes. 'How shall I put this? There are three members: a retired fireman, a berry farmer and a filling station owner . . . not an educator among them . . . so I took it on myself to make that decision.'

'What post did you hold before you came here?' I ask.

'You're confusing me with these irrelevant questions. What does this have to do with the hit and run?'

'The manner of death hasn't been established yet.'

'This is all very puzzling,' she says. 'I don't know what you want from me.'

'I haven't forgotten my question, Miss Hanover.'

'I taught at Saguaro Correctional out in the Mojave if you must know.'

'That's the girls' reformatory,' says Jim.

'Yes, it was an opportunity to make a difference in the girls' lives.'

'But?' I say.

'It's a little embarrassing. I'd planned to remain longer, but the isolation was too much for me. Believe me, officers, if you've seen one cactus you've seen them all.'

'That your Dictator parked outside?'

'Oh, heavens no,' she says. 'It's on temporary loan from a family friend.'

I ask her for a list of the students and she complies. 'Please, bring the children in,' I say.

When they're seated, I ask if anyone saw Georgie after class on Friday. A few saw him walking with Kenny but that was it. Rebecca Smallwood sits silently with arms crossed over her chest. Her eyes flick toward the teacher, then back to me, and I wonder if she's conveying a tacit communication. It's obvious that her relationship with Miss Hanover is strained, so it's not the right time to single her out for questioning.

'We may need to speak with you again, Miss Hanover,' I say. 'If you recall anything further please give us a call.'

I fold the list of student names and addresses and slip them in my notebook. I turn to Miss Hanover and nod toward the blackboard. 'I'm just a cop, ma'am, not an educator like yourself, but I believe you misspelled 'misspell'.'

Her mouth opens and her head swivels toward the blackboard. I wink at Rebecca Smallwood on my way out the door and she hides a smile behind her hand.

Jim and I walk up to the Dictator. It has an impressive vertical grill, crank windshield, sloped trunk, graceful hood ornament and art deco instrument panel. 'What do you think something like this costs?' asks Jim.

'Don't ask me. I can't count that high.' I open the car door and check out the registration strapped to the plastic sleeve on the steering column. 'It belongs to Ludwig Gerhard von Buchholz.'

'That's a mouthful,' says Jim.

'Know who he is?'

'Never heard of him. What's his address?'

'Five Twenty Upper Cork.'

'That's the St. Ambrose Hotel. Pretty fancy digs. By the way, she's watching us from the window.'

★   ★   ★

On our drive back to town Jim glances over at me. 'You got something on your mind?' I ask.

'You were hard on her, Jack.'

'I know. Angel tried to enroll Albie Sherman in Orchard School. Hanover made up some phony excuse and turned him away. He's a good little kid, Jim. Truth is, he wasn't white enough to suit her.'

'There's a lot of that going around. Listen, why don't I call my Uncle Pete and take him out to lunch. He's the retired fireman on the school board. I'd like his take on the new school teacher.'

'Good idea.'

'But just because you don't like her doesn't mean she's done anything wrong.'

18

Cookie has never had so many crippling headaches without a clear vision presenting itself. Anxiety at the loss of her precious elixir is making things worse. She's furious with Joe for sticking his nose in her business. Then there's the withdrawal from the narcotic that made the golden liquid so . . . so . . . she had to admit it . . . habit-forming. She's damned if she does and damned if she doesn't.

Last night another fragment of the puzzle took shape — a little girl peering from behind a row of collapsing sunflowers at the back of the schoolyard. She knows it's not the child's face she needs to see, but what the girl is looking at, and that part refuses to come into focus.

If Cookie's vision hadn't been so full of holes, she'd be on the phone with Jack Dunning. Then again, what's unclear to her might make sense to him. With weary steps she makes her way to the phone, sinks onto a kitchen chair and dials the station.

'Sergeant Green here,' comes the voice on the other end. 'How may I help you?'

'Hello, Bruce. This is Cookie. Is Jack in?'

'Sorry, Cookie. He's tied up on a case right now.'

'Does it have something to do with Orchard School?'

'I know he was out there this morning. You want to leave a message?'

'I don't know if I can leave one that makes sense.'

'Another vision?'

'Not a very good one. I can explain it better to Angel. By the way, how is Curley coming along?'

'He's home from the hospital. I'll tell him you asked.'

Cookie hangs up and redials. When Hank answers she asks for Room 210.

★ ★ ★

Leland walks into Community Bank at 10:30 a.m. He should have arrived

181

sooner, but he had a bad night and overslept. When he woke, Frances was gone and he didn't see Sahara Princess in the pasture.

'Good morning, Mr. Dietrich,' says the teller.

'Good morning, Miss Starling.'

'Lovely morning. I was beginning to wonder if we'd ever see the sun again.'

'Me too,' he says. 'I'd like to close my account if you don't mind.'

She glances at his checkbook. 'You mean the joint checking?'

'Yes, Miss Starling, the joint checking.'

'Sir, Mrs. Dietrich has already done that for you.'

'I beg your pardon?'

'Five minutes sooner and you would have bumped into her. The checkbook you're holding is obsolete.'

The earth shifts beneath him and he feels faint.

'Are you alright, Mr. Dietrich?'

'Yes, yes of course. I simply didn't think she'd have time today. Since I'm here, I'd like to access my safe deposit box.'

'Did you bring your key?'

'Yes, I have it right here.'

'I'll take that,' she says.

'What do you mean?'

'Frances had hers too. Everything has been transferred to Citizens Bank in Manteca. Since we'll have to reassign the box, we can't have an extra key floating around now, can we? Mr. Dietrich, are you listening?'

His body is numb. He can't think. He drops the key in her hand.

'We hate losing you as customers, but you know how Mrs. Dietrich is when she gets the bit between her teeth.'

'I do indeed.' Her stupid colloquialisms make him want to jump over the counter and choke her until her eyes pop out, but instead he smiles miserably. 'I'm having serious reservations about a check I issued on Saturday. I'd like to put a stop payment on that.' He refers to his checkbook. 'Here it is, check number 4705.'

'It cleared just minutes before Mrs. Dietrich got here. I remember because we don't see a draft in that amount every

183

day.' She gives him a sympathetic smile. 'Well, what can I say? The early bird gets the worm.'

He flees the bank in a dissociative fugue, dropped onto a street he's never seen before, in a town he's never been to. Frances has cut him off and his passport now sits in a safe deposit box in Manteca. He stumbles into an alley between two brick buildings, puts his hands against the wall and throws up behind the garbage cans. Little by little his mind and body reconnect and his air of imperial insouciance slips back into place. After several minutes he straightens his tie, wipes off his shoes and steps from the alley. He buys a newspaper and reads it in the car.

Photos of the fire are all over the front page, an inspector being sent from San Francisco to determine the cause. Leland had no idea that torching an old building belonging to a few ragtag Jews was going to cause such an uproar. In Germany's current political climate, making an issue over such trivia would be a crime in itself. Much to his relief, there's nothing in the article about a body being discovered in the ashes . . . yet.

Dietrich is suddenly struck by a brilliant idea. He'll ask Hansel von Stroheim to return the donation he made to the Deutschlander Club. He thought the money would make a favorable impression, help him move up in the organization and achieve some of the glory that his father had attained in the Great War. His heart aches for home. There's nothing to hold him here, but first he'll need money and traveling papers. As the Americans say so colorfully: It's time to get the hell out of Dodge.

★ ★ ★

Jim returns to the squad room after lunch with Uncle Paulie. We face one another, the backs of our desks pushed together. 'No one on the school board knows about Georgie's demotion,' says Jim. 'He passed all of his tests last year and deserved to be promoted. Miss Hanover is obviously not a team player.'

'The board may never have known that if the Geiger boy hadn't spoken up. I'd like to know what her former boss has to say about her, wouldn't you?'

'There's the phone,' says Jim.

The operator patches me through to Saguaro Correctional as Jim listens on the other line. A secretary answers and puts me on hold for the head administrator. It's a good minute before he picks up.

'Churchwell here.'

'Mr. Churchwell, this is Detective Jack Dunning with Santa Paulina P. D.'

'Yes Officer, how may I be of assistance?'

'I'd like employment confirmation on a Miss Penelope Jane Hanover. Her résumé puts her in your employ last year.'

After a slight hesitation: 'Yes, that's correct.'

'Can you give me a brief run-down for the record?'

'She taught English. She was well-liked and left of her own accord a few weeks before final exams. Is she all right?'

'Yes, she's fine.'

'Well, that's a relief. Her mother has been terribly worried. She hasn't heard from her since she left Saguaro. Perhaps you could encourage her to give her family a call.'

'I will. Where do they live?'

'Culver City. It's down in Los Angeles County.'

'How would you describe Miss Hanover?'

'Early twenties. Medium brown hair. A plain but pleasant face and modest attire. She always wears a large cameo at the collar of her blouse. She's a bit naïve and bubbly.' Jim and I look at one another with raised eyebrows.

'What reason did she give for leaving?' I ask.

Again, the hesitation. 'I can't say for sure. She didn't give notice. One morning she was simply gone. It isn't the first time an employee couldn't adjust to the remoteness of Saguaro. Knowing she's safe gives me hope our missing students are safe as well.'

'What missing students?'

'Three runaways. Flyers are still up in the border towns, but the sheriff isn't that interested in pursuing the case.'

'I imagine they'll surface eventually.'

'That's what he says.'

'One more thing. You say Miss Hanover taught English. How would she have spelled 'misspell'?'

'With two esses of course. You'd never trip her up on that one.' I sense that he has more to say but holds back. We talk a few more minutes and hang up.

'Her story checks out,' says Jim. 'She taught at Saguaro like she said. She also fits the physical description. But naïve and bubbly aren't the first words that come to mind.'

'I agree.'

I slide the files of Georgie Allen and Danny Battle across the desk. 'Would you please go over these again? I've looked at them until I'm blue in the face. Homer believes Allen and Battle were killed for the same reason. If Georgie was suffocated, Platt thinks the Battle boy probably was too. There were no signs of molestation on either child and the adult motives of jealousy, greed or revenge certainly don't apply.'

'So what am I supposed to be looking for?'

'If I could answer that I'd find it myself.'

'Maybe the killer just likes killing, and who's more easily killed than kids? If we find the person responsible for Georgie's death, we'll know who killed Danny Battle — unless, of course, he really was the victim of a hit and run.'

Jim takes an hour picking through the photos and files, but can't find any connection other than the boys having gone to the same school and being found at the same location. We divide the list of students down the middle and go off in separate cars. We spend the afternoon interviewing kids and their parents. When Mrs. Smallwood opens the door, she has a black eye and a bruise on her arm. She says Rebecca is 'out somewhere' and closes the door.

So what have I learned? Not much. Georgie is quiet. He has one friend. He has cooties. He's been demoted to a lower grade. The teacher seats him at the back of the room.

It's late. Jim calls it a day and goes home. I'm beginning to think about food when the phone rings. 'Lieutenant Dunning, here.' No response. I hear soft, hesitant breathing — a child's breathing. Only one person comes to mind. 'Rebecca?' I say. 'Is that you?'

A male voice: 'Put down that phone or I'm getting the switch!' There's a click and the phone goes dead. I look the Smallwoods up in the book and dial their number, but no one picks up. While I have the book out, I notice the ad for the St. Ambrose Hotel. A phone in every room. A bathtub in every two-room suite. I lean back in my chair and dial the number.

'St. Ambrose Hotel.'

'This is Detective Jack Dunning.'

'Yes, Detective Dunning, how may I help you?'

'Who am I speaking with?'

'This is Henry at the reception desk.'

'Henry, would you please ring the room of Mr. Ludwig von Buchholz?'

'I can ring the room, sir, but it wouldn't do any good. Mr. von Buchholz is traveling on the *Queen Mary*.'

'What's his room number?'

'On the *Queen Mary*?'

'At the St. Ambrose.'

'That would be 423, sir.'

'Ring it, please.'

'One moment, sir.' I listen to ring after ring. Henry comes back on the line. 'Sorry, sir. Would you like to leave a call-back number?'

'Did he say when he'd be back?'

'I have no information to that effect.'

'But he hasn't forfeited the room.'

'That's correct.'

★ ★ ★

I push my hunger aside, grab my hat and head for the car. It's dark when I pull onto Cleveland Street, a run-down block of shabby houses just this side of the railroad tracks. The sidewalks are buckled and the street lights shattered. The house is a narrow two-story building rented by the room. Half of the gingerbread trim is missing and the third step leading to the sagging porch is lying in the weeds. I knock on the frame beside the screen door. It's a good two minutes before a

191

middle-aged woman waddles to the door. She has blonde hair with black roots, dirty elbows and a cigarette clamped between nicotine-yellow teeth.

'Stella Bloch?' I say.

'Who wants to know?'

'Detective Dunning.'

'You're wasting your time, mister. I run a clean house here.'

'I'm sure you do. Is Miss Hanover in?'

'Who?'

'Penelope Hanover, the schoolteacher.' There's a vacancy behind the eyes. 'She rents from you.'

'Oh, her. I remember now. She won't be in until late. I believe she's at the library correcting test papers.'

'Is that the same place she'll be if I call again tomorrow and the day after that?'

'What's that supposed to mean?' she says, throwing her weight onto a lumpy hip.

'Can you show me which room is hers?'

'I can't do that. I'd need either her permission or a search warrant.'

'I'll just stand in the hall while you open the door. I won't even go in.'

'Sorry, the ladies are bathing. Men aren't allowed inside the premises after dark.'

I bet. Everyone is lying to me, but I don't know why.

19

Don Swackhammer considers himself monumentally over-qualified for the position of mail carrier. After all, he was with the S.P.P.D. for three years before his forced resignation on trumped-up charges of dereliction of duty. If it weren't for his Uncle Mort on the city council, he'd be working the late shift at the packing plant.

He sure does miss those lazy Sundays at the station, kicked back with his girlie magazines, his feet on the desktop. Hardly a call would come in all day; everybody at church or too hung over to move after a night in Santa Paulina's watering holes.

Today he gets to drive the truck around town, collecting mail from the big curb-side boxes. It's sure a sight better than humping the heavy leather bag from door to door with nasty little dogs savaging his ankles. He pulls up to the box on St. Finnbar Street and accesses the security door. He finds a dog-eared notebook among the stamped letters. A ring of keys slides to the ground. Swack opens the notebook. Inside are scribbled notes. Times. Dates. Places. Initials. It's common practice for people to drop lost items down a mail slot, so he puts the book and keys in the truck with the rest of the mail.

Further up the block he stops in front of the rubble that was once the synagogue. Even before it burned it was a blight compared to the neat bricks and manicured lawns of St. Finnbar's. Swack has strict orders not to leave his vehicle except to collect mail or go to the diner for lunch. All right, so one day he stopped at Bunny Mifkin's for a nooner and the unattended mail bags were ransacked. Big deal! It's not like he went to sleep on guard duty and terrorists blew up the Denver Mint.

Curious, Swack looks around, gets out of the truck and approaches the rubble. It's quiet on the street, classes in session and no one in sight. The heaped piles of ash pulse with heat, like the building clinging to its last vestige of life.

He looks once more to make sure the coast is clear, then walks through the lot to the back. He kicks at the ashes, wondering if there's money in the ruins, or religious artifacts of silver and gold. Everyone knows Jews pretend to be poor while they hide fortunes in cash and jewels. Maybe he'll come back and dig around when the site cools off.

In the rubble is a leather shoe curled with heat. He nudges it with his foot. Ashes rise in a powdery cloud and slowly resettle. He bends over and pokes the melted heel with the butt of his jack-knife. It's attached to something. He crouches down for a better look. It's an old dog bone. No — it's an ankle bone, and the ankle bone is attached to a leg, and the leg is . . .

Swack jumps up with a frightened yelp and runs for his truck.

★　★　★

Frances is back at the house by one o'clock. She goes to her room, calls the Pinkerton Agency in San Francisco and asks for Mr. Andrew Culver, Singleton's superior.

'Mr. Culver, this is Frances Dietrich calling from Santa Paulina.'

'Yes, Mrs. Dietrich, I know who you are.'

'Has Darrell Singleton checked in with you today?'

'No, he hasn't. As a matter of fact we were about to call you.'

'I haven't heard from him. I'm afraid the investigation has turned into something more complicated than surveillance of a cheating husband.'

'Like what?'

'I'll have to get back to you on that.' She hangs up before he can formulate his next series of questions. The phone rings, but she doesn't pick up. It won't be Singleton, now or ever.

★ ★ ★

At three thirty that afternoon, the electrician has completed his work and climbs the stairs from the basement on Hilliker Road.

'You're all set up, Mrs. Dietrich.'

'I'd like to pay now. Any objection to cash?'

'I prefer it.'

He names his price and she throws in an extra twenty.

'You look like a man who knows how to keep his mouth shut,' she says.

'Lady, I wasn't even here.'

* * *

Leland needs to make a phone call. He decides on the indoor booth at the Tammany Hall Bar, noisy with blue-collar Irishmen, the slap of dice cups and click of pool balls. They can't hear one another over the racket, let alone eavesdrop on a telephone conversation.

He orders a whiskey straight and gets a handful of dimes and quarters from the bartender. Inside the booth he pulls out von Stroheim's number. Long distance. Los Angeles. He finishes half the drink before he gets up the nerve to dial.

'Yeah, Hansel Von Stroheim here.'

'Hansel, this is Ludwig,' he says,

keeping his voice sunny and casual, just two friends shooting the breeze.

'Yes, Ludvig, ve had a very successful first meeting, no? You vill be very important asset to da Deutsch-American Bund,' he says, breaking into his native tongue. 'The generosity of your donation is being spoken of all da vay to da top.'

'Yes, well that's the reason for my call.'

'I can barely hear you, Ludvig.'

'What I'm saying is, I'm going to need that money back — the donation money — just for a while, you understand.'

Silence. The operator comes on the line and he shovels a few more coins into the machine. There's a chill on the other end of the line.

'Hansel, are you still there?'

'You vant back da money? I cannot be hearing correctly.'

'Yes, as soon as possible, actually. I've gotten myself in a bit of a jam, but in a month or two I can double the donation and we'll both be ahead of the game.'

'Certainly you understand, it's not *my* money to give back. Already it has gone up da chain of command. To ask for it

199

back vould be a great embarrassment to me.'

'Would you consider a personal loan? I'll have it back to you in sixty days.'

'I cannot believe vut I am hearing.'

'Listen, I've already done the Bund a great service. I've initiated our racial policies here in Santa Paulina. My cousin and I are both dedicated to the cause.'

'I have no idea vat you're talking about.'

'The synagogue fire. It's all over the front page. I'm surprised you haven't heard.'

'You fool! Da first meeting of da Club and already a fire to incriminate us? Have you lost your mind, Ludvig? You have no authority to act unilaterally. You vill ruin da mission for everyvon.'

Dietrich is stunned. 'I thought you'd be pleased. We want to drive out the Jews, right? Eliminate the inferiors?' He thumps his forehead against the phone booth and sits through another drawn-out silence. 'Hansel, don't make me beg.'

'I must do some thinking.'

'I hope that means you have my back

on this. I want to go home. I will need a new passport.'

'All dis is not so simple. Dere are people I have to answer to. Call me back tonight, let's say around 2:00 a.m. By den I may have solution.'

20

Early darkness erases the last of the orange and violet sunset from the sky. I drive toward the Rexford with both Georgie's and Danny's files on the seat beside me. I'm so preoccupied with the case, I'm not sure how long I've been driving behind the yellow Auburn. I snap to attention, follow it down Cork, and into the lot behind the St. Ambrose Hotel.

The driver gets out of the car. He's tall, white-blond, expensively shod and tailored like a character from the pages of *The Great Gatsby*. I park, wait a few minutes, then follow him inside. Until now I had no idea what Dietrich looked like and I'm pretty sure he doesn't know me.

When I enter the Gold Dust Lounge, he's sitting at a table against the far wall. The room is deeply carpeted and softly lighted. I take a stool at the bar where I can watch him in the smoked-glass mirror in front of me. I order a gimlet. Dietrich looks nervous. He lights a cigarette and keeps running his fingers through his hair. The cocktail waitress brings him a bourbon.

Ten minutes later a statuesque young woman walks past me toward Dietrich's table. She wears a black satin dress with a glittering gold belt, strappy high heels and a stylish red hat. She sits across from Dietrich facing the room, a veil with velvet dots obscuring the upper half of her face.

Dietrich lights her cigarette, her scarlet fingernails catching the light from the candle on the table. The waitress brings her a drink with a paper umbrella in it. Dietrich leans forward as he speaks, like he has something of great urgency to impart. She stiffens and shakes her head. Whatever it is, she's not going for it.

'Who's the lady?' I ask the bartender.

'Who wants to know?'

'Jack Dunning, Santa Paulina P.D.'

'I thought you Irish hung out on Lower Cork?'

'They ran out of little pink umbrellas.'

He pops a laugh. 'She's the school-teacher. Has a suite on the fourth floor.'

'St. Finney's?'

'The one in the orchard.'

I study her more closely, mentally stripping away the veil and the scarlet war paint on her lips.

'Jesus, don't tell me that's Penelope Hanover.'

'Ever know a teacher who looked like that?'

'I've never known *anyone* who looked like that. Is she his mistress?'

'His cousin, from what I've heard.'

Hanover rises so quickly the back of her chair strikes the wall. Whatever he said has really pissed her off. I look away as she exits the lounge, leaving her drink untouched. She takes the elevator to the fourth floor. The woman looks like she's made of money. I pay for my drink and station myself outside the alley door.

Two cigarettes later, the door opens and Dietrich steps into the dim glow of the exit light. I snap an elbow into his face and hear the cartilage snap in his nose.

He stumbles back against the wall. I follow with a blow to the solar plexus and a rabbit punch to the back of his neck. It felt good, really good, maybe not to him, but to me. He's on his knees, his hands trying to catch the blood that dribbles from his nose onto his cashmere coat. I grab his collar and pull him to his feet.

'My wallet's inside the coat,' he moans.

'I don't give a damn about your wallet, Dietrich. This is about Angel Dahl. I don't know what you did to her, or how long ago, but I have a pretty good idea, you unmitigated pervert. You ever come near her again and I'll kill you. If I catch you in Little Ireland, I will gun you down like a dog in the street. Am I getting through to you? Am I?'

'Yes, yes, I get it.'

* * *

Dietrich stumbles onto the seat of the Auburn. He never dreamed that so many things could go wrong in one day. Now that he's in hot water, his cousin wants nothing more to do with him. She's

205

certainly not going to lend him money, and she refuses to return the Dictator. Frances has stripped him of his assets, von Stroheim has his money, and some guy with a fist like a rock just beat his head in. He drives toward Hilliker Road, the last place in the world he wants to go. If von Stroheim comes through for him, he'll be out of the country in a day or two and his troubles will be over.

* * *

When I enter 210, Angel comes out of the bathroom in her terrycloth robe and greets me with a hug. I breathe in the scent of Ivory soap and the clean smell of her hair. I touch my hand to her forehead.

'The fever's almost gone,' she says, 'and I can hear out of my ear again. I missed you so much today.'

'I'm sorry I'm late. There's a lot going on at the station. Homer thinks both of the boys who were found on the road are homicides. The motive is staring me in the face, but I can't see it. I'm sorry. I don't mean to drag the job home. It'll take me a minute or two to unwind.'

Angel strokes my hair. 'It's all right, Jack. You'll figure it out. You always do. I saved you a couple of hamburgers from the café.'

'Great, I'm starved.'

I set the boys' files on the windowsill beside a big bouquet of flowers. She hangs my coat in the closet and pours me a cup of coffee. I sink into the easy chair and attack the bag of hamburgers. Angel takes the chair across from mine.

'Jack, you have blood on your jeans.'

'I wonder how that got there. I'll take them down to the wash.'

'You're not hurt, are you?'

'No, I'm fine.'

'You don't want to talk about it?'

'It's not important.'

She studies me in silence for a few beats. 'Cookie called today.'

'How are her headaches?'

'Bad right now.'

'She really needs to see a specialist.'

'I know. She's having visions again, something about the one-room school-house. She made me promise to pass

207

along what she told me. It didn't make a lot of sense really, something about the teacher at Orchard School.'

I wolf down the first hamburger. 'I'm listening. What about Orchard School?'

'In her dream, the teacher was dressed all prim and proper, but when the wind blew her skirt up, there was a bright red petticoat underneath, the kind can-can dancers wear.'

'What did she make of it?'

'She says Miss Hanover isn't who she pretends to be. She's one person on the outside and another person underneath. In the dream, she was dancing with a lunch box. I know it sounds silly, but I promised I'd tell you.'

'A lunch box. I'll give that some thought. Anything else?'

'She saw a girl in braids peeking from behind a row of dead sunflowers, but she wasn't able to see what the girl was looking at.' I finish the second hamburger and toss the napkin in the waste basket.

A girl in braids. Could be Rebecca Smallwood. 'Let me sleep on it.' I stand and feel the weakness in my bad hip. I work a knot out of my back. 'Where did the flowers come from?'

'Albie brought them up. They're from Tom Kelly, along with a get well note.'

After a pause, I say: 'Tom Kelly is interested in you, Angel. I think you should know that.'

'Interested in what way?'

'In *that* way. He asked me if he could take you to the movies.'

'But we're together, Jack. I don't understand.'

'Neither does he. He thinks I'm your father.'

'I'm so sorry, Jack. What did you say?'

'Nothing. I walked away.'

'I'll throw the flowers out if it makes you feel better.'

'Please don't. Flowers aren't the problem. Let's face it — he has a lot more to offer you than I do. Another few years and I'll be one more over-the-hill cop and you'll still be young and beautiful. You can do better. I know it and so do you. I see your opportunities slipping away one by one. I look at myself and I don't like what I see.'

'Please don't say that, Jack. I'll talk to him.' She studies me with those blue-as-rain eyes. 'If you're trying to get rid of me, you'll break my heart. If you are, just tell me.'

'Get rid of you?' I put my finger beneath her chin and turn her face toward mine. 'I plan to die in your arms,' I say, pulling her close. 'That proves what a selfish bastard I am.'

★　★　★

When I come out of the shower the next morning, Angel is in the easy chair looking at the photos of Georgie Allen and Danny Battle, two small, fragile bodies on ice-cold slabs.

'I'm sorry, I should have left those in the car,' I say. 'You don't need to see all this bad stuff.' She continues to study the photos. Finally, she looks up.

'I think I see the connection,' she says. 'I know why they were murdered. I'm not saying it makes sense, but look.'

I stare at the photos. 'What? I don't see it.'

'Georgie Allen had head lice, right? With his head shaved the scabbing is visible on the photo.'

'That's right.'

'Now, look at Danny Battle. The boy is covered with some kind of rash. There's blistering and inflammation all over his arms and legs. It's either eczema or psoriasis. It itches. Kids scratch it. It bleeds. It can be an unpleasant distraction to other people, especially if they think it's contagious.'

'I don't know what you're getting at.'

'Remember how Miss Hanover wouldn't let Albie enroll in her class? She doesn't think he's good enough to mix with white children. Dark skin. Head lice. Eczema. Don't you see the pattern, Jack? These children are being systematically weeded out of the gene pool and that teacher has something to do with it. We're lucky she turned Albie down or he might have ended up in the ditch too. This is exactly the kind of thing Nathaniel Forsythe has been warning people about on his radio show.'

'It sounds terribly far-fetched!'

'That's because we don't think the way

some people do. In her philosophy the genetic race goes to the swift and the strong with no room for imperfection.'

★   ★   ★

Leland Dietrich steals up the back stairs to his room, unwilling to be seen with his broken nose, his eyes black and blood dripping down the front of his coat. He washes up and begins collecting valuables to hock at Sal's Pawn Shop: two jewel-movement watches, diamond cufflinks, matching tie clip and new set of golf clubs. Now he wishes that he hadn't gone into Chinatown and let Fu Gang rob him blind. They could at least have waited until he got his money's worth.

At 2:00 a.m. he picks up his bedside phone and calls von Stroheim, who's in a far better mood now that he's had a chance to think things over.

'Yeah, yeah, your money you can have back, but vill take a vile to get in order, including passport. Day after tomorrow, ve'll meet across bridge on River Road and I vill hand over. Midnight vould be good time. No vorry, is all taken care of, my comrade.'

Dietrich breathes a sigh of relief. 'Thank you, Hansel! Thank you! Heil Hitler!'

21

The next morning, Jim wakes up with an abscessed tooth and won't be in until later in the day. I bring my files up to date, then put in a call to Amos Duncan, who picks up on the third ring.

'Dunk, it's Jack Dunning.'

'Hi, Jack. How you doing?'

'Hanging in there. Could you have Hayden or Priscilla call me? I have a question for them.'

'Priscilla's right here at the kitchen table. Hang on a minute.' Priscilla comes on the line.

'How are you and Hayden holding up?' I ask.

'The best we can, Officer Dunning. How is the investigation going? Have you found out anything new?'

'We're following a few leads, Priscilla. I'm sorry things aren't moving faster.'

'Hayden and I want to thank you for what you're doing. I want you to know we're going to be okay. We know our boy is safe with the Lord. Mr. Duncan is getting us train tickets back to Cutter's Gap. We want to bury Georgie in the family plot.'

'Dunk is a good man. Has Mr. Platt returned Georgie's possessions to you?'

'He has, but there was nothing worth saving.'

'Was anything missing that should have been there?'

'Only his black lunch box. It's adult size, the one his daddy took down in the mines back in West Virginia.'

'And he had it when he left for school that last morning?'

'Yes. Is that important?'

'It could be. When are you leaving?'

'Day after tomorrow. We'll leave our address with Mr. Duncan so you can reach us. Back home we're five miles from the nearest phone, so write and we'll get back to you.

I dial the Geigers' house and Kay picks up. 'Mrs. Geiger, this is Officer Dunning. How is Kenny doing?'

'Improving. We're not going to tell him

215

what's going on until he's feeling better.'

'Would you ask him something for me? Did Georgie have his lunch box with him the last time they were together?'

She steps away from the phone. I hear muffled voices and she comes back on the line. 'Yes, he had his lunch box when they ran into the orchard.'

'Thank you, Mrs. Geiger.'

If his lunch box wasn't found in the orchard or the ditch, what happened to it, and where is it now?

★   ★   ★

A sweaty, sunburned young man in a Model T leaves a two-mile trail of dust in his wake as he speeds through the gates of Saguaro Correctional and skids to a stop in front of the administration building. He asks to make an emergency phone call and due to his state of extreme agitation, receptionist Margie Springer summons Horace Churchwell to the lobby.

Churchwell introduces himself and asks the man his name.

'Calvin Parvine, sir. I just come from

rock climbing in the Alamillo.'

'If you tell me the nature of your emergency we may be able to assist you. It'll take the sheriff a good two hours to get out here. If he's tied up it could take longer.'

'Best I just show you what I found, then.'

Calvin opens his backpack, pulls out a few items of clothing and turns it upside down. The receptionist stifles a gasp as a skeletonized hand adorned with a garnet class ring spills onto the desktop. A small Star of David on a tarnished silver chain lands on top of it.

'That looks like Miss Hanover's ring,' says Margie, 'but that's not poss . . . oh, my god!'

'Steady, Miss Springer. Steady now,' says Churchwell. 'Take a couple of deep breaths. Where did you find these, Calvin?'

'At the bottom of a crevice, where all the skeletons are.'

'Margie, call the sheriff, then find the number of that detective out of Santa Paulina. Dunning is not dealing with

Penelope Hanover. He's dealing with Hedy Greiss.'

* * *

Frances isn't feeling well so Mittie spends the night in the guest room. She lies awake into the wee hours, listening to Frances cough and pace the floor. At eight thirty she brings her coffee and a croissant and at nine o'clock she's back with an armload of clothing.

'What in the world is that god-awful smell?' says Frances, looking up from the morning paper.

'These were in the garbage can, Mrs. D. They're Leland's clothes and they're soaked with gasoline.'

'Gasoline? Leland wouldn't pump his own gas if you held a gun to his head.'

Frances pours a second cup of coffee and unfolds the newspaper on her breakfast tray. An unidentified body has been found in the ashes of the synagogue. Frances has a very bad feeling in the pit of her stomach.

On the front page is a photo of Cantor

Nemschoff being interviewed in the lobby of the Rexford by a reporter from *The Sun*. He's quoted as saying that everyone from the synagogue has been accounted for. When he's asked if arson for profit might be involved, he throws his hands up in dismay. The old relic was uninsured and uninsurable.

'Do you want me to toss the clothes out?' asks Mittie.

'No. Bag them and put them in the tack room for now.'

'I heard Mr. D. in his room last night. He left before I got up this morning.'

'Good.'

When Frances looks at Mittie, it's obvious the girl's potential is far beyond that of her current station. Who would have thought that in the end, her closest friend and confidant would be a lady's maid?

'What is it, Mrs. D? You look worried.'

'I'm losing you, Mittie.'

'Only as an employee, not as a friend. I'll *always* be here for you, Frances.'

'You said that young man of yours passed the bar.'

'Yes, ma'am.'

'What's his name?'

'Nehemiah Goldman.'

'Mittie Goldman. Yes, it suits you well. Got a good business head on him, does he?'

'The best. He'll be practicing corporate law.'

'You set a date for your wedding yet?'

'We're thinking June would be nice.'

'Sooner would be better. Make it a Christmas wedding, Mittie. I'd like to be there.'

★ ★ ★

Jim comes in at about eleven, his jaw swollen and his mouth stuffed with cotton. First I tell him about Cookie's vision and then about Angel's theory.

'I can't absorb that right now. The gas the dentist gave me has deadened my brain.'

'Try to absorb this one thing. I saw Penelope Hanover at the St. Ambrose last evening. The man she met in the lounge was Leland Dietrich, husband of Frances

O'Hara of bootleg booze fame.'

'You think they're getting it on?'

'According to the bartender, they're cousins. She looked like a high-class hooker — black dress, scarlet lipstick, skyscraper-high heels. She lives in Suite 423 and she reeks of money.'

'If I had to reek of something, money would be *my* first choice. Did you check out the house on Cleveland?'

'I don't think she's ever lived there. She just doesn't want people to know she's living in luxury at the St. Ambrose. It would ruin her schoolmarmish image.'

'What do you think is going on?'

'I think she's the mistress of von Buchholz, the man who owns the Dictator. As we speak, he's sailing on the *Queen Mary*, but we can question him when he gets back. Hanover certainly can't afford that suite on a teacher's salary. The woman's a chameleon and boy can she change colors!'

Jim laughs around the ball of cotton in his cheek. 'Okay, so she turns from a pumpkin into a tomato when the sun goes down, but what bearing does that have on our case?'

'I'll be damned if I know. Let's pay another visit to the school. I want to know what became of Georgie Allen's lunch box.'

'What lunch box?'

'Come on, I'll explain on the way.'

As we exit the squad room we find ourselves walking elbow to elbow with Sergeants Boyle and Green. 'You look like you're going to a fire,' says Jim.

'In a sense we are,' says Boyle. He holds up a notebook and a key ring. 'Swack brought these in this morning. They were in a mailbox down the street from the synagogue.'

'And?'

'Haven't you heard? An anonymous caller reported the body of a man in the ashes. Chief Garvey and the fire inspector are down there now. We're thinking the notebook and keys might belong to the dead man. There was blood on the sidewalk near the school and a spent cartridge in the grass. Now we're going to look for the car that belongs to these keys.'

'Any name in the notebook?' I ask.

'It's pretty cryptic — mostly initials, dates, that kind of thing.'

'Well, good luck.'

'You guys still working the Allen case?' asks Green.

'We are,' I say.

'Give yourself a break. It was a hit and run.'

Jim and I are halfway out the door when Sergeant Duggan waves a message slip and calls my name.

'When I get back,' I call over my shoulder.

I wouldn't know until later that it's an urgent call from Saguaro Correctional.

22

Penelope Hanover stands in front of the class. She's not pleased to see us, but manages a tight smile. 'You'll have to come back another time,' she says. 'I'm dismissing class for the day.'

'Why so early?' I say.

'I'm not feeling well. I'm going home.'

'We only need a few minutes of your time.' I stand in front of the blackboard and Jim stands beside the shelves in the cloak room where the children's lunches sit in a row. I address the class. 'One by one, beginning with the lowest grade, I'd like each of you to collect your lunch and return to your desks.' There are several sack lunches, children's lunch boxes and three large black ones like the one belonging to Georgie.

'What on earth are you doing?' says Miss Hanover, a nervous flush rising to her cheeks. 'This is highly irregular.'

After a few minutes every lunch but

one has been claimed. The black boxes belong to older boys, each with their names painted or scratched into the metal, none belonging to Georgie. Two lunchless girls in bare feet and faded flour sack dresses sit with their hands folded and eyes lowered.

'The remaining sack lunch has no name on it. Who does this one belong to?' I ask the teacher.

'I can't imagine,' she says. 'It must be left over from yesterday.'

'That's Rebecca's,' pipes a boy in the back row. I'd already noticed her absence. Miss Hanover gives me a chilly look of inquiry. 'Why are you here?' she says. 'What is it you want? I've already answered all of your questions.'

'Georgie Allen owned a lunch box. It isn't here,' I say. 'It wasn't in the orchard and it wasn't in the ditch. So where is it?'

'What does it matter? He had it when he left.' She realizes her mistake the minute it comes out of her mouth.

Jim smiles. He looks like a squirrel with a cheek full of nuts. 'You said you had no memory of him leaving that day, remember?'

'I'm simply assuming. He always carried it with him.'

'Now we have Rebecca's lunch and no Rebecca.'

'She came to school with the flu. I sent her home, but not before she passed it on to me. I'd keep your distance if I were you.' Whether intentional or not, it sounds like a threat.

'You seemed in the full bloom of health in the Gold Dust Lounge last night.' It comes and goes quickly from her face — a flash of fear. A few children giggle at the thought of their mousy teacher in a hotel bar. I turn to the class and clap my hands together. 'Okay kids, go on home.' The children grab their coats and fly out the door. As soon as we're alone her anger simmers to the surface.

'All right, Lieutenant,' she concedes. 'So, I'm a real person with a real life after the factory whistle blows. It is now a sin to look fashionable?'

Her change of syntax doesn't go unnoticed and I'm not quite sure what to make of it. 'Don't get me wrong, Miss Hanover. You looked smashing. It's just dramatically inconsistent with the way you present yourself to the world. It makes me wonder which is the real Miss Hanover. Both of them? One of them? None of them?'

'I'm not feeling well. Can't we do this tomorrow?'

'I had a talk with Horace Churchwell.' At the mention of his name she stiffens. 'Why so nervous? He confirmed everything you told us about your term of employment, even the reason for your departure. What you failed to tell us, however, is that you left before the end of the semester.'

'It was irrelevant.'

'By the way, how is it you can afford a suite at the St. Ambrose? Family money? A lucky hand at poker? The mysterious Ludwig von Buchholz? I've talked with Mrs. Bloch on Cleveland Street. Would you care to comment?'

'You've certainly done your homework, Officer Dunning, but I've committed no chargeable offense.'

'It's actually *Detective* Dunning. We're a curious breed, especially when we think someone isn't being entirely candid with us.'

'I don't know what you're talking about. My life is an open book.'

'Your life is a book of secrets, lady.' A tic pulls at the corner of her left eye and she breaks eye contact.

'Unless you're going to arrest me for having a nice hotel room and fancy clothes, I'm leaving now,' she says. 'If you have further questions you can address them to my lawyer.'

'By the way, Churchwell wants you to call your mother. She's worried about you.'

'It is a mother's job to worry.'

'He wants to know if you still have her San Diego phone number?'

'Yes, of course.'

'You haven't done *your* homework, Miss Hanover. Your mother doesn't live in San Diego.'

She brushes past us out the door. We watch her start up the Dictator and drive toward town.

'Let's check on Rebecca while we're here,' I say.

We drive up Schoolhouse Road to Rebecca Smallwood's house and knock on the door. A goat peeks around the corner of the house and bleats a greeting. No one answers and there's no car in the driveway.

'Maybe her mother took her to the doctor,' says Jim. 'What if she really does have the flu?'

* * *

Frances pulls the ceiling chain and a dim light goes on at the top of the basement stairs. She brushes aside cobwebs and descends the steep flight through a rush of cold air smelling of dust and stored apples.

The moment she looks at the recording device on the main phone line, she knows it's been activated. Her heart thumps in her chest as she rewinds the tape and turns the knob to play. She listens for thirty seconds, turns it off and lets fly a barrage of profanity worthy of Red O'Hara. She coughs until her throat is raw. She knows what she needs is on that tape, but the conversation is in German.

'Mittie!' she calls up the stairs, her voice rattling with gravel. 'Come down here and bring my cigarettes.'

There's a quick, light tread on the stairs. 'Here you are,' says Mittie, handing her a pack of Old Golds. 'What are you doing down here, Mrs. D? It's freezing.'

'Remember the cantor in the morning paper, the one who said he was from Berlin?' She taps a cigarette from the pack and lights it, her hand a little unsteady.

'Yes, Cantor Nemschoff.'

'See if he'll come here. I need a translator.'

'If he had a car, I don't think he'd be limping around the neighborhood on a cane.'

'Take the Mercedes. If he balks, offer him a bribe.'

'What kind of a bribe?'

'Whatever it takes.'

★ ★ ★

I pick up the message slip from my desk blotter. It's Horace Churchwell's private extension. Jim and I get on the line and I dial. Churchwell picks up on the first ring like he's hovering over the phone.

'Horace, this is Jack Dunning returning your call,' I say.

'Jack, I hardly know where to start. All hell has broken loose around here. The Alamillo Escarpment is crawling with cops.'

I lean forward in my chair. 'What's happened?'

'A hiker discovered four skeletons up there.'

'Four!' An incredulous look passes between Jim and me.

'Yes, four skulls and miscellaneous bones.'

'What the hell is going on?'

'We suspect three are the missing students. A skeletonized hand was wearing Penelope Hanover's class ring. She's probably been dead since May. I think your teacher is Hedy Greiss, an embezzler from our accounting department who vanished a week before the arrival of the state auditors. We have reason to believe she's murdered all of these people, but to what advantage, I can't imagine.'

'I may know the answer, Horace, but I'll have to get back to you on that.'

As soon as we hang up, the phone rings. It's Mrs. Smallwood, Rebecca's mother. 'Yes, Mrs. Smallwood. How may I help you?'

'I was returning from town when I noticed there's no one at the school. Where is everyone?'

'The teacher sent the children home.'

'Then, where's Rebecca?'

I snap to attention. 'Miss Hanover said she went home with the flu.'

'That's nonsense. She was perfectly well when she left this morning.'

Rebecca, the curious little girl who saw something from her hiding place behind the sunflowers.

'Do you know if she tried to call me yesterday?' I ask.

'We thought she was calling a boy. Her father made her hang up the phone. Why? What's going on? Where is she?'

'I'll get back to you on that, Mrs. Smallwood. I have to make a few inquiries.' I hang up before she asks questions I have no answers for. I look at Jim. 'We need to get to the St. Ambrose. I think Hanover is about to bolt, and she might have Rebecca with her . . . if the girl is still alive.'

* * *

Mittie helps Cantor Nemschoff down the basement stairs, one slow step at a time on his feeble knees. Frances stands restlessly by as the cantor listens to the tape, rewinds it and listens a second time. When he's finished, Frances switches off the machine.

'Two men talking,' he says. 'Day vill meet tomorrow at midnight on River Road across bridge. Dah von calt von Stroheim is bring money and passport to dah von called Ludvig. Dat is vat you vant to know, correct?'

'Correct. Thank you. You understand that everything you've heard here is confidential.'

'I do.'

'I'm only gathering evidence for a court case, nothing more.'

'Is not my business.'

'You've been a great help,' says Frances. 'How can I compensate you for your time?'

The cantor makes a broad sweep of his hand, indicating she is a rich woman who has much to be thankful for. An abacus clicks inside his head as he quickly calculates the value of his silence.

'I have in mind you should perform a little mitzvah,' he says, and whispers in her ear.

Frances rolls her eyes. 'That's what I was afraid of,' she says, but she smiles when she says it.

* * *

I drive and Jim rides shotgun as we fly down Cork St. to the St. Ambrose Hotel. The Studebaker Dictator is not in the lot. I'm already flipping my shield as we trot up to the clerk at the front desk.

'We need entry to the suite of Penelope Hanover,' I say.

'There is no room registered to a person of that name.'

'Room 423.'

'I imagine you have a search warrant,' he says, looking down his nose at the blue-collar cops from Little Ireland.

'You can imagine anything you please,' says Jim, poking the bloody cotton back in his cheek. 'Just hand over the goddamn key or I'll strangle you with your tie.'

The concierge rushes over. 'Henry, Miss Hanover checked out half an hour ago,' he says. 'Give them the key.' With a prissy two-fingered gesture, Henry drops the key into Jim's hand.

'Remember when we talked on the phone and you deliberately misled me, Henry?' I say. 'When I get back we're going to have a nice little chat down at the station.'

'Well, I . . . I . . . '

I turn to the concierge. 'Did Hanover have a young girl with her?'

'No, sir; just a purse, one suitcase and her passport. I glanced at it when I removed it from the hotel safe. It was her photo, but the name didn't fit. It was something like Heidi Geist.'

'Hedy Greiss.'

'Yes, that was it. Did you know she was here from Germany?'

'I know now.'

I'd grown suspicious back in the classroom when she'd said, *So, it is now a sin to look fashionable?* People under stress often slip into the syntax of their native tongue. A small lapse, but very telling.

Once inside 423 we see the expensive wardrobe and luxurious accessories left behind in haste: furs, jewelry, Lalique perfume bottles, pieces of white luggage monogrammed in gold — luxuries that were probably purchased with money embezzled from Saguaro Correctional or given to her by Leland Dietrich. In the left corner of the closet is her teacher's wardrobe of grey and black skirts, high-collared blouses and low-heeled practical shoes.

'Look what I found in the closet,' says Jim. 'A shortwave radio. She's some kind of foreign agent.' We drag it into the room.

'That's even better than a skeleton.' It's when I see the black lunch box in the back of the closet that my blood runs cold. I pick it up. It has H. A. for Hayden Allen scratched into the paint. I'm looking at a souvenir taken from the murdered child.

'Here's another one,' says Jim, lifting a smaller plaid lunch box from the closet shelf. Written on a piece of adhesive tape inside the cover is the name Danny Battle. We're looking at mementos of unspeakable deeds perpetrated on the weak and defenseless.

'The chief needs to put out a BOLO for the Studebaker,' I say. 'My bet is she's heading south to L.A where she can get a rail connection to the east.'

'Not if we can help it,' says Jim.

We tape off the room and race back to the car.

23

Hedy Greiss swings the Dictator behind the schoolhouse. She takes a hammer from the trunk, walks behind the bed of sunflowers and whacks the lock off the outhouse door. Rebecca lies on the floor, drugged, bound and gagged.

The girl makes a chipmunk sound in her throat when Hedy pulls her up by the hair and tosses her in the trunk. In seconds she's traveling south in her black hat, leather coat and shiny boots. Somewhere between Santa Paulina and Los Angeles, she'll pull off the road, wrap the brat's mouth and nose with tape and toss her in the underbrush. Once she gets to New York she'll book passage on a steamer bound for the Fatherland.

She can't wait to get out of the US, although she's enjoyed dispatching a few mongrels and defectives along with the nosy teacher whose identity she's assumed. She'd have taken care of the little colored boy too if she hadn't run out of time. Soon there will be another great war. The Aryans will establish dominance over all inferior races and she will have been a part of it.

Hedy passes through small towns and miles of orchard and vineyard, white-knuckling the wheel, eyes locked in a purposeful trance. Although a lower profile vehicle would best serve her at the moment, the Studebaker can dominate the road at a steady forty-five mile clip.

About an hour out of Santa Paulina, she pulls into a small station in the middle of nowhere and cranks open the windshield to let in some fresh air. From the office, the attendant squints at the car and goes for the phone. She can't believe those hick cops have already put out a be-on-the-lookout.

She pulls a Luger from her pocket, strides through the office door, shoots the attendant in the head and jerks the phone cord out of the wall. A car approaches from a distance and with no time to gas up, she continues south, her gas tank running low.

Hedy feels rhythmic thumping through the floorboards. Rebecca is conscious and kicking. She slams on the brakes and pulls to the side of the road, stomps to the back of the car and throws the trunk open. The girl has slipped her bonds and removed the gag. She's also pulled the lining back from the floor and ripped out several electrical wires.

Rebecca struggles violently as she's pulled from the trunk and sinks her teeth into her captor's thumb. Hedy screams with pain but Rebecca only grinds deeper until she hits the bone. Hedy strikes her in the head with her fist, but it isn't until she cocks the gun and jams it against her temple, that the girl lets go. Hedy staggers backward with a moan and sucks on her wounded thumb.

Her immediate impulse is to shoot the kid, but she gets her emotions under control. A quiet kill is better, like the wet towels she pressed over the faces of Danny Battle and Georgie Allen. The boys were dirty . . . contaminated. She recalls with disgust the nits and lice, all that scratching and ooze. The solution was simple. Offer a hungry kid a nickel candy bar and they'll get in a car with the devil herself.

As for Rebecca? It's not that she saw much, but it's enough to contradict everything Hedy told Dunning and Tunney. And now the bite. She's never felt anything so painful. It's already swollen to twice its normal size, and the bacteria from human teeth can be deadly.

A flatbed loaded with bales of hay is coming from the opposite direction, and she doesn't want some chivalrous hayseed stopping to ask if she's having car trouble. Hedy shoves Rebecca in the front seat and pulls back onto the highway.

Hedy tries the headlights, but all that wire-pulling has disabled them, along with her plan to drive non-stop through the night. She aims for Rebecca's face with a sharp backhand, but the kid hunches down and takes it on the arm. The car is bucking and stuttering when she pulls into the next station, a crumbling adobe box in the middle of nowhere with quake fractures running up the walls. She turns to Rebecca.

'If you make a sound I will shoot the attendant, then blow your brains all over the front seat. Understand?'

Rebecca, her face stained with tears, her braids in a tangle, nods her head. Hedy is sweltering inside her leather coat. She tosses it, along with her hat, into the back seat, freeing an abundance of wavy brown hair. She slips her Luger in her slacks pocket and looks around at the two rusty pumps sitting on a pad of cracked concrete. No phone lines run to the building.

The attendant is a woman . . . sort-of. She's Mexican, about five feet tall, with a gut like a five-gallon drum and a pack of hard muscle at the shoulder . . . short bristly hair . . . a thin cigar in her mouth. A defective! A mongrel! Hedy tries to hide her disgust. The name embroidered above the creature's pocket reads 'CiCi'. She has a welcoming smile and axle grease under her fingernails.

'You want I should fill 'er up, señorita?'

'Please.'

Cici removes the gas cap and stretches out the gasoline hose.

'May I use the phone?' asks Hedy, to

make sure there is none.

'A storm took the lines down, but you can make a call at the general store half a mile up the road.'

Confirmation. No phone. Maybe she'll let this one live. Hedy sees Rebecca eying the car keys and jerks them out of the ignition with a scathing look. Rebecca has seen her parents drive enough times to know how it's done. What if the car couldn't move at all?

With Hedy's eyes on the attendant, Rebecca works one of the tiny buttons loose at the collar of her dress. With a tug it pulls away from the material. She holds it between her fingers and forces it deep into the key slot.

Hedy pays for the gas and climbs back in the car. Sitting on a full tank, she breathes a sigh of relief. She goes to insert the key and looks puzzled when it won't go in. She tries again and bends over for a closer look. Now she panics, wide-eyed with terror, her eyes cutting toward Rebecca. 'What have you done?'

Rebecca bolts from the car.

'Help me!' she hollers. 'I've been

kidnapped! She's got a gun!'

Hedy climbs from the car and goes for the Luger. Her swollen thumb gets in the way and she fumbles the gun. Startled, but quickly sizing up the situation, CiCi swings the hose in her direction, pulls the trigger and drenches Greiss from head to foot with gasoline. Hedy manages to stabilize the gun in a rather awkward grip and aims it at the attendant, finger on the trigger.

'Stand back!' CiCi shouts, but Rebecca's already running away from the car. CiCi flicks her cigar onto Hedy's sweater. There's a loud whoosh and she ignites like a Roman candle, her hair flashing, then shriveling like melting plastic around her head. She shrieks, spinning and gyrating in a macabre dance toward the road. She drops, rolls and thrashes wildly, then goes motionless on the gravel shoulder . . . like Danny . . . like Georgie . . . like road kill.

Mongrels, one.

Master race, zero.

CiCi hangs up the hose with a shaking hand and trembling knees. 'Saints preserve us!' she says. This is far more excitement than she expected when she rolled out of bed this morning. She gives the flaming puddle on the ground wide berth and approaches the girl.

'You okay, my little *muchacha*?' she says.

'Not really,' says Rebecca, her hazel eyes as big as moons, tears cutting through the dust on her cheeks.

'Well, you will be. What's your name?'

'Rebecca Smallwood. I'm from Santa Paulina. I want to go home.'

'Rebecca. That's a good, strong name. Look at me. I'm as fat as a Shetland pony. Who do you think can reach the general store quicker, you or me?'

Rebecca wipes her tears and takes off down the road to find help.

★   ★   ★

Jim and I stop when we see an ambulance at a service station in Stanislaus County north of Turlock. A deputy tells us the attendant has been murdered, but we should keep going, because there's something even bigger going on just this side of Merced.

When we arrive, the second scene is crawling with deputies, a coroner, and a growing crowd of curiosity-seekers in cars and pickups, on horseback and on foot. The Studebaker sits in front of a gas station and on the side of the road, covered with a canvas tarp, is a lump too small to be a cow and too large to be Rebecca Smallwood.

We compare notes with the local sheriff and bring one another up to speed. He tells us about the quick-thinking station attendant . . . a woman, no less . . . who torched a kidnapper and freed the hostage. Jim and I are ecstatic. CiCi Gonzales has done everything for us except write our report. The Studebaker stays in Merced as part of the criminal investigation and after giving a statement, Rebecca is released into our custody.

On the drive home, Rebecca tells us that she didn't witness the murder of Georgie Allen, but she saw Greiss lure the boy from the orchard into her car, never to be seen alive again. We're disappointed that she won't face the American judicial system but there's no doubt as to her

246

culpability in at least six homicides. Our first call when we get back to Santa Paulina will be to the Allens. Their son's case has been solved.

Georgie was killed because he was poor and had head lice, Danny because he had a chronic skin condition. I will learn in the next few days that Patty Gregson had a disfiguring birthmark and Velma Becker, a stammer. Sarah Levin was killed simply because she was Jewish. But it was Hedy Greiss who had the biggest defect of all: a cruel, black heart.

As for CiCi Gonzales? Tomorrow she'll be on the front page of every newspaper from San Francisco to Los Angeles. Rebecca deserves to be there too, for her bravery and quick thinking.

I take the wheel as we leave the daylight behind, Rebecca asleep in the back, Jim dozing in the passenger seat with a big lump on his jaw. Things don't always work out exactly the way you plan them, but you take what you can get, any way you can get it.

24

For the first time, Joe walks alone into senior night at St. Finnbar's. The charred smell from the synagogue fire next door lingers in the night air. It's an awkward moment, standing alone without Cookie at his side. If he smoked he'd light a cigarette to calm his nerves.

Like most men, Joe is not a big talker. That was Cookie's job — a natural-born chit-chatter. She could break the ice in a room of mortal adversaries by reading their horoscopes and palms. She'd make everyone laugh by studying a life line and telling someone they'd passed away three years before.

Tonight the high school gym is a ballroom, festooned with red and green crêpe paper and bouquets of shiny balloons. The air smells vaguely of Old Spice and Evening in Paris, with ladies wearing their prettiest dresses, the men sports coats and dress shoes. Father Doyle circuits the room with his hands joined behind his back, nodding greetings and making sure no Protestant infidels from the Baptist Church have crashed the festivities. Nuns smile and serve punch and oatmeal cookies at a folding table along the wall.

People ask where Cookie is and Joe is hard up for an answer. Until tonight it's been Joe and Cookie, Cookie and Joe. How can he tell them he stole her pain medication and she's dumped him? He mingles, he dances, he pretends to have fun, but all he wants is to go home to Pumpkin and feel sorry for himself.

He decides to have a glass of punch, then slip out the door. Bing Crosby sings 'Pennies from Heaven' on a scratchy record, followed by a big band number. He finishes his drink and tosses the paper cup in the wastebasket. From the corner of his eye he sees Ginger Everly weaving toward him through the crowd. Once he's made eye contact, he can't pretend he didn't see her. Tonight she wears a sunny yellow party dress, matching high-heeled shoes and an eager smile too big for her face.

'Rescue me, Joe,' she says, touching his arm. 'One more toe-crusher with Hughie from the feed store and I'll be crippled for life.'

'I don't dance very well,' he says.

'It's a Sin to Tell a Lie' spins on the turntable. 'Come on, it's a slow one.' She pulls him to the center of the floor. He moves his weight listlessly from one foot to the other. 'So, where's Cookie?'

'She's at home.' This time he's prepared . . . sort-of. 'I only drove down to look at the burned-out synagogue. I really need to get back and let the cat out.'

'Liar, liar, pants on fire!' she says. 'You two are on the rocks. Everybody knows it. She cancelled Effie Mosely's reading twice this week. Effie says Cookie is so depressed she can't get out of bed. You're better off without her, you know. You're a successful businessman and she reads fortunes for ten cents a pop, for god's sake!'

'I don't see it that way.'

'Oh come on, Joe. Let's go to my place for a nightcap. I've got some great Benny Goodman records.'

Joe doesn't answer. He's staring over her shoulder at the door.

'Joe, did you hear what I said? You're Italian, right? I have a nice bottle of Dago red chilling in the fridge.' She turns to see what he's looking at. Cookie stands across the room in her matching red coat and hat, looking every bit as lost as Joe feels. 'Oh my god, I can't believe it!' says Ginger. 'The woman's come in pink bunny-ear bedroom slippers.'

'She has arthritis,' says Joe. 'At the end of the day shoes hurt her feet.'

Cookie scans the crowd and their eyes meet.

'How embarrassing,' says Ginger. 'Just ignore her and maybe she'll go away. We can sneak out the back.'

'Ginger, please stop talking.'

Cookie covers half the distance between them, then stops like she might turn and run back out the door. Joe turns to Ginger. 'Please excuse me,' he says, releasing her. He looks back at Cookie and closes the gap between them.

'Well!' says Ginger, and she walks off.

'I'm sorry, Joe,' say Cookie. 'I'm sorry I

251

took you for granted and kept you hanging all these years. It wasn't right.'

'No, *I'm* sorry, dear. I had no business stealing your devil juice. You can have it back. I didn't have the heart to throw it out. And I'll never pressure you about marriage again.' He gives her a big, warm hug. 'I missed you so much.'

'I missed you too, Joe. Ask me again.'

'What?'

'Please, ask me again.'

There's a flash of recognition on his face. 'Will you?' he says, his face brightening.

'Yes, I will.'

★ ★ ★

Cantor Nemschoff lies awake late into the night listening to wind rattle the window. The strange conversation he heard on the recording plays over and over in his head. He wishes Raisel were still alive so they could discuss it over a glass of schnapps. He hates being old and alone, and now that the synagogue is gone, the gravity that tethers him to earth grows weaker.

He can't help speculating about the

men on the recording, what they're up to and how it involves a rich lady like Frances Dietrich. The one called von Stroheim speaks like a native German, probably a Berliner like himself. The one called Ludwig? He's not so sure. He sounds more like an Englishman, fluent in the German language. They talked money. A very large sum of money. Transactions of that size are generally handled at the bank or a lawyer's office.

Noah Solomon Nemschoff was not born yesterday. He knows that honest men transact business in the light of day, not down by the river at midnight. He should tell Jack Dunning what he knows and how he knows it. Then again, he promised Frances Dietrich to keep his mouth shut. It is a dilemma for which he could use the opinion of a Talmudic scholar. Tonight, he will sleep on it. He has one more day to decide what is right.

★   ★   ★

A call from the desk wakes us around 9:00 a.m. and Angel picks it up. I groan and roll over in bed, my shoulders stiff from the long drive, my bad hip grinding nerve on bone.

'Hank needs you in the lobby,' says Angel. 'He says come as you are, but come quick.'

I throw on my robe and slippers and limp half-asleep to the elevator. Albie and Bo are in the lobby. A stout woman in a hat decorated with cabbage roses is trying to pull the dog out of his arms by its ears. She's yelling, Albie is crying, and the dog is squealing like a stuck pig.

I throw my hands up. 'Hey, hey, hey! That's enough. Let go of the dog, ma'am.'

The woman lets go and looks at me. 'Who do you think *you* are?' she says.

'Law enforcement.'

She looks me up and down, me with my morning bed-head, bristly face and road-weary eyes. 'You don't look like a cop.'

'I forgot to pin the star to my pyjamas. And you are?'

'Isabel Gross, LuLu's sister from Carmel. Since Roland is stuck in that cast, we're not bothering with a funeral. I've simply come for the interment and to retrieve my dog.'

'Roland Barker give me this dog, Mister Jack. You heard him with your own ears. He's mine fair and square,' says Albie, sniffling and brushing at his tears. Bo looks at me with his bat ears, jagged under-bite and bulbous eyes. He's the most pitifully unattractive animal I've ever seen.

I address Mrs. Gross. 'I know you want the dog, but what's your *legal* claim?'

'I paid $35.00 for Bo when he was a puppy. He was a birthday present for LuLu. Now that she's gone, I'm taking him back.' She reaches once more for the dog. Bo cowers and nips her hand.

'That little monster!' she says. 'I think he's drawn blood.'

'Ma'am, the dog doesn't want to go with you.'

'All he needs is a firm hand.'

'Once you gave LuLu the dog, you gave up possession. When she passed away, he became the property of Roland, her next of kin.'

She huffs a laugh. 'That's hogwash. That man can't even take care of himself.'

'That's why he gave the dog to Albie,

and it was his right to do so. You can see they've bonded and Bo is well taken care of.'

'If he keeps my dog, I want the money back.' She crosses her arms over her ample bosom, a battleship at anchor.

'I have $17.00 in my coffee can and you can have it,' says Albie.

'A dog is not a car that depreciates when you drive it off the lot, young man,' she says.

I turn to Hank, who's shaking his head and observing from behind the desk. I'm still sitting on the proceeds from the sale of my Boston house. 'Hank, would you please get $35.00 out of the safe?' He spins the dial, pulls the lever and counts the money out on the counter. The woman's eyes light up when she sees the crisp bills. I hand them over and she can't slip them in her purse fast enough.

'Satisfied?' I say.

'I suppose I'll have to be.'

'When's the interment?'

'This afternoon. Two o'clock. I'm leaving right after the service.'

'Good. Have a safe trip.'

25

After a hectic week, Angel and I draw back into the center of our lives. We lounge around the hotel room in our night clothes, smoking, talking, making love. When I watch her brush her hair or smoke a cigarette or put on her earring, I feel like I did on the night we met, a love so intense my chest aches. I want to touch her, taste her, bury my face in her hair. Call it obsession, I don't care, but having Angel in my life is like finding a treasure I don't deserve at the end of a long journey. She catches me watching her and smiles like she's reading my mind.

Toward evening, Jake knocks on the door and tries to reimburse me for the cost of the dog. I won't take it. It's an early Christmas present for Albie, I tell him. We call Cookie to see if she'll join us for dinner. Getting no answer, we kidnap Hank and the five of us pile into the Caddy and go to the Memory Lights Café for fish and chips, leaving Bo snoring on the floor by the heater.

By 11:30 we're back in the room feeling warm and contented. Angel and I are getting ready for bed when Cantor Nemschoff knocks on the door. He crooks his finger and asks me to step into the hall. After we talk, I come back into the room and Angel sees the change in my demeanor. I get dressed, check my gun and strap on my shoulder holster.

'Jack?' she says.

I pull on my boots and sheepskin jacket.

'Jack, what is it?' I see the alarm on her face.

'I don't know yet.'

'You're scaring me,' she says. 'Call Jim. Whatever it is, please, don't go alone.'

'There's no time.' I put my hands on both sides of her face and kiss her on the forehead. 'Get some sleep. I'll be back as soon as I can.'

★　★　★

I position myself back in the trees where River Road intersects with the highway, leaving my car on the town side of the bridge in front of the Blue Rose. Down the hill from where I stand the river is swollen and dark. I don't have to wait long before a black Mercedes backs into River Road and stops. The headlights go off. I can't make out who's behind the wheel.

Almost simultaneously two more cars enter my field of vision: a black sedan driving in my direction from the highway and Leland Dietrich's yellow Auburn from across the bridge. Both pull off the road a few feet beyond the intersection. The man in the sedan switches off the headlights and gets out. Dietrich gets out and leaves his headlights on.

'Good evening, Hansel. It's good to see you again so soon.'

'Turn off your lights, Ludvig,' says the man. Ludwig? Leland Dietrich is the illusive Ludwig von Buchholz? 'Vee don't need to advertise.' Hansel is a tall, imposing figure, with a thick-as-strudel German accent. I hear a soft click as the door of the Mercedes opens and a shadow moves closer to the intersection.

'I prefer a little light on the situation,' says Dietrich.

'Vat happened to your face? You valk into a freight train?'

'Very funny. Do you have the money?'

'Yeah, also I have passport. Is no vay to tell from real thing.' He reaches into the breast pocket of his overcoat as Dietrich approaches. Instead of money he withdraws a gun.

'What do you think you're doing?' says Dietrich. 'Do something foolish and you will answer to my father.'

'You are loose cannon, Ludvig. You have acted vithout higher authority, potentially drawing negative attention to our organization at a sensitive time. A murder? A fire? All for ego? Vee must now close down club for Deutschlanders. All money and energy on project vasted. You may think you are superior to everyvone, but you are not your father, Ludvig, and I am acting on his instructions. Vord comes back to him you are corrupter of children and women. You are abuser. Is disgrace on family name.'

'Just wait a minute, Hansel. I'll go

home and speak to him. There's no real damage done and we can make all this go away like it never happened.'

Gun drawn, I make my way through the trees, about to intervene, when Frances Dietrich steps to the edge of the light in her jodhpurs and riding boots, and without a word, plugs the tall German in the head with one expert shot. The gun falls from his hand and he buckles to the ground without a sound. Astonished, Dietrich spins toward his wife, his face pale as chalk, his mouth agape.

'Frances! Where did you come from? My god, you just saved my life.'

'Not really,' she says. 'Here's one for Red.' And she sinks a bullet into his chest. He looks in disbelief at the red flower blossoming over his heart. He crumples to his knees, then onto his face. Frances Dietrich has just blown away two men as casually as most women cut a tea cake. I was a little slow to react, but what the heck? Looks like it was a one-woman job.

'Okay, Mrs. Dietrich, hold it right there,' I say. 'Drop the gun.'

She pivots and sprints back toward her car, coughing hoarsely, snapping off bullets in my direction. One hits the tree about three inches from my ear. As she peels out I pump three slugs into the trunk of her car. I don't intend to shoot her. I just want to be able to prove she was here. I'd failed to identify myself as S.P.P.D. She probably thought I was just another anonymous threat.

I check both men for vitals. They're dead. There's no need to rush as I walk back over the bridge. I call Jim from the Blue Rose. I call Chief Garvey at home. He says he'll be right down with the coroner. We seal off the perimeter. The press shows up. Flashbulbs explode. The Chief says we'll make a formal statement in the morning after we sort things out.

After the scene has been processed and the bodies taken off in the bread truck, I go back to the station to type up my report. Frances Dietrich sits at my desk, having a smoke, her gun on the desktop in front of her. If she'd intended to shoot me, I'd have been dead when I walked through the door.

'Hey, Frances, what's up?'

She laughs and coughs in the same breath and I see blood on her lips.

'Sorry, Dunning. I didn't know it was you at first.' She sets a tape on my desk. 'Get out your pencil,' she says. 'I'm going to spill my guts.'

After taking a formal statement and scrutinizing the notebook belonging to the Pinkerton detective, everything falls into place: Dietrich shooting Singleton . . . Dietrich torching the synagogue . . . Dietrich's affiliation with the German Bund. After three hours, I'm seeing double. I set my pen down, close my notebook and exhale.

'Just for the record,' she says, 'I shot von Stroheim to protect my husband and I accidentally shot Leland in the process. You know how inept we women are with firearms.' I try hard as hell not to smile. Her story could be hard to *disprove* and I'm not exactly going to go into mourning over a child rapist and a low-level Nazi. 'If you have a problem with that,' she says, 'book me so my lawyer can bail me out and I can go home and get some sleep.'

For all of thirty seconds, I'm engaged in a moral tug of war.

'I'll hang onto the gun,' I say. 'Go home, Mrs. Dietrich.'

26

The refurbished dining room at the Rexford opens just in time for Cookie and Joe's wedding reception. The room is decorated with carnations and red poinsettias. There are candle globes on the tables, good restaurant china, sparkling glassware and shining silver plate. The long buffet table is spread with golden roasted chickens, mountains of wild rice, artichokes and Brussels sprouts trucked in from Castroville, and dozens of potluck dishes. The centerpiece is a white four-tiered cake decorated with frosting roses that Joe baked himself, and in the front window of the lounge is a Christmas tree full of tinsel and lights.

Now that the dining room will be open for nightly meals, Agnes Peel and two other women from the housekeeping staff have been reassigned to kitchen duty as dishwasher and assistant cook. Angel oversees the operation, plans the menus and acts as hostess. Tonight she wears a tailored powder-pink suit with a string of dime-store pearls, her hair swept off the nape of her neck in a honey-blonde swirl.

'You've got your dining room.' I say. 'You pulled it off.'

She smiles. 'I did, didn't I?'

'I imagine Cookie will be moving into the big house now,' I say.

'That's what I thought too, but Joe's going to sell it. He's moving into the apartment with Cookie. He'll be right above the bakery and she'll be able to continue reading fortunes. They're honeymooning in San Francisco so Cookie can consult with a headache specialist.'

'Let's hope something works this time.'

'Did her clue pan out? You know, the one about the little girl by the sunflowers?'

'It did. It's uncanny. I don't know how she does it.'

'Neither does she.'

With dinner over, everyone is circulating with cups of coffee and slices of cake, young and old mixing together, the elderly shut-ins come out of their shells. Roland is out of his cast and spinning around the room in a wheelchair.

'I'm so happy, Jack,' Angel says. 'This is my home and these people are family.'

'Marry me, Angel.'

She searches my face. 'You were the one with reservations,' she says. 'What's changed?'

'I was afraid of letting you down.'

She touches my cheek. 'You could never do that. You're the one who gave me my life back, remember?'

'Is that a yes?'

'Jack, I said 'yes' the night we walked to the Rexford in the midnight rain. I've been saying 'yes' ever since.'

Jake and Albie join us, as does Bo, with velvet reindeer antlers on his head.

'Albie, do you ever smell good,' says Angel.

Albie giggles. 'That's not me, Miss Angel! That's Bo. Roland give me LuLu's bottle of coconut shampoo and I give him a bath. Hank says he smells like the fancy girls at Candy O'Toole's boardinghouse.'

'I better not catch you going near *that* place,' says Jake. 'Go show Bo the Christmas tree so us grown-ups can talk.' As he walks away I can see the pride on Jake's face. 'Next month he starts school, first little colored boy at St. Finney's. I'm still trying to visualize him in his green blazer and Irish plaid tie. Gives new meaning to black Irish, don't it?'

'I'm way ahead of you Jake. I see him on a scholarship to Notre Dame.'

'Everybody, everybody, come quick! Hurry, hurry! It's snowing!' cries Cantor Nemschoff.

Everyone piles into the lobby. Big flakes of snow are wheeling through the haloes of streetlights, silvering the holiday decorations strung from pole to pole above the street. We follow the crowd outside and watch the snow collect on the sidewalk and rooftops.

'Have you ever seen anything more beautiful?' says Angel.

'It hasn't snowed here in thirteen years,' says Hank. 'It's a good omen. Maybe we'll live long enough to see the end of the Depression.'

'I guess this is the big one we've been waiting for,' says Roland, his wheelchair spinning circles on the sidewalk.

The cantor stands next to us, leaning heavily on his cane. 'Did you hear the news about the synagogue?' he asks.

'Tell us,' says Angel.

'A secret benefactor is building us a new one. Construction starts as soon as the plans are drawn up.'

'That's wonderful news. Congratulations.'

Albie looks up at the snow swirling past the face of the moon and spins in dizzying circles. Bo races up and down the sidewalk, snapping at the flakes and sliding on the slippery concrete. Tom pulls up to the curb in his cab and lets out a fare. I walk over.

'Tom, get inside and grab a piece of cake. There's plenty of food left too.'

'You sure, Jack?' he says, a trace of uncertainty in his voice.

I smile and give him a friendly clap on the shoulder. 'I'm sure, Tom.' He nods and goes inside.

Joe and Cookie come through the door in their traveling clothes. We cheer and throw rice as they pull away from the curb in Joe's big car.

'You want to go up?' says Angel. 'I'd like to get out of these shoes.'

I know what that means and I don't

269

need a second invitation.

We slip away from the crowd and take the elevator to the room. The lights are low, the pink and purple neon from the theater flickering across the ceiling. When I turn back into the room Angel is in her slip, her hair tumbling soft and golden over her shoulders. I put my arm around her and she leans into my side. We stand in silence and watch the snowflakes blow past the window. I'm happier than an alcoholic over-the-hill cop has a right to be.

I tap two cigarettes from the pack. When I take out my lighter, Angel takes it from my hand and sets it on the lamp table with a smile. She looks up at me with eyes bluer than rain . . . a little more than kitten . . . a little less than cat. She takes my hand and leads me to the bed.

I still know how to make her purr.

THE END

We do hope that you have enjoyed reading this large print book.

Did you know that all of our titles are available for purchase?

We publish a wide range of high quality large print books including:
Romances, Mysteries, Classics
General Fiction
Non Fiction and Westerns

Special interest titles available in large print are:
The Little Oxford Dictionary
Music Book, Song Book
Hymn Book, Service Book

Also available from us courtesy of Oxford University Press:
Young Readers' Dictionary
(large print edition)
Young Readers' Thesaurus
(large print edition)

For further information or a free brochure, please contact us at:
Ulverscroft Large Print Books Ltd.,
The Green, Bradgate Road, Anstey,
Leicester, LE7 7FU, England.
Tel: (00 44) 0116 236 4325
Fax: (00 44) 0116 234 0205

Other titles in the
Linford Mystery Library:

ROSE POINT

V. J. Banis

Karen marries Alan Denver and returns with him to the cliff-side house next to the lighthouse he tends. However, she knows nothing of the death — or even the existence — of his first wife. Then she begins to sense strange ghostly presences about the house, and her husband starts behaving oddly. She senses, too, that Alan's mother, who lives nearby, is trying to break up her marriage — but why? The truth lies hidden behind a locked door, and in a scrap of rose point lace . . .

THE CORPSE IN CACTUS

Lonni Lees

The murder that Detective Maggie Reardon has solved at a local Tucson art gallery creates unforeseen difficulties in her personal life. Then, to complicate matters, a corpse is discovered at a museum lying under a bed of cactus. What at first appears to be a tragic accident quickly starts to smell like murder. Maggie's been dealt a nameless victim with no witnesses, no suspect, and no apparent cause of death. And as the evidence unfolds, she must also battle a hostile fellow cop, determined to see her lose her badge . . .

MISSION OF MERCY

John Robb

A revolution breaks out in the independent Arab republic of Hanah. The French legation is in danger. A tiny Foreign Legion detachment is sent into the country, ordered to protect European lives and property. But that detachment is in no condition to undertake a task that calls for restraint as well as courage. It is under the command of Captain Laubert, a cunning but demented officer . . . a man who has been threatened with arrest by his junior officer.